BIRTH OF MAGIC

A SUN-BLESSED TRILOGY NOVELLA

CAROL BETH ANDERSON

Birth of Magic by Carol Beth Anderson

Published by
Eliana Press
P.O. Box 2452
Cedar Park, TX 78630

www.carolbethanderson.com

Cover Design:
Front cover, exclusive of text: Carol Beth Anderson
All cover text plus spine and back cover: Mariah Sinclair (thecovervault.com)

Edited by Sonnet Fitzgerald (sonnetfitzgerald.com)

Paperback ISBN: 978-1-949384-03-1

First Edition

BE AN INSIDER!

Insiders get updates on Carol Beth Anderson's books, plus early cover and title reveals, notifications of sales, and more. Sign up at carolbethanderson.com.

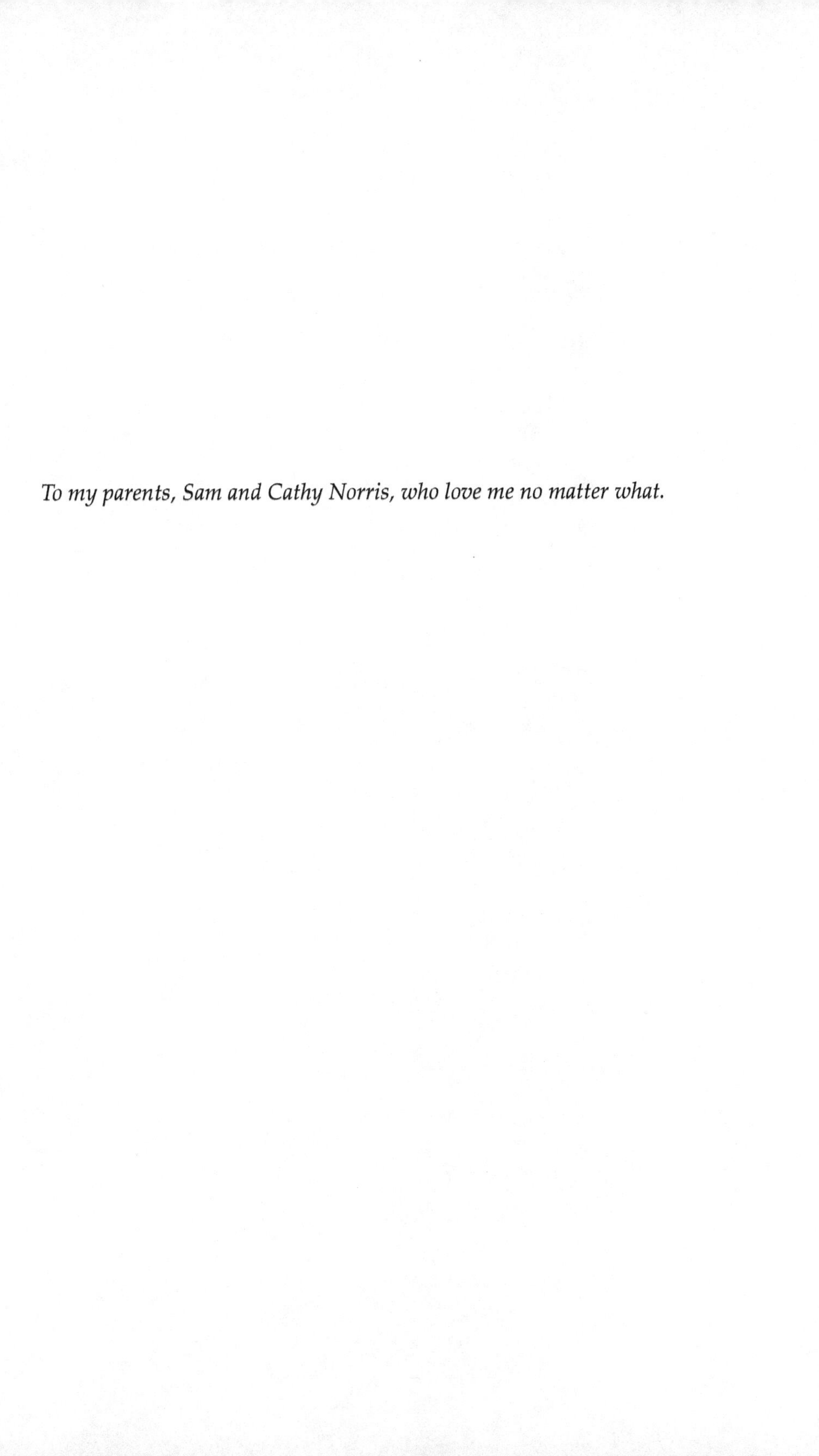

To my parents, Sam and Cathy Norris, who love me no matter what.

CHARACTERS AND PLACES

Characters

Edoren (EDD-oh-ren) the Bard
Alena (Uh-LAY-nuh)
Alaya (Uh-LIE-uh)
Kari (KARR-ee)
Jenki (JENN-kee)
Havadom (HAV-uh-dom), goes by Dom
Mara (MAH-ruh)
Roza
Yolin (YO-lin)
Savala (SAH-vuh-luh)
Rusk
Mayor Held
Mrs. Held

Places

City of Esherin (ESH-er-in)
Esherin House

CHAPTER ONE

How did magic—that benevolent, untamed force—first enter the world?

I have traveled to a dozen lands and have heard twice that many versions of this story. To begin, I shall relate the tale my grandfather told me.

Generations ago, how many I know not, humanity was on its deathbed. Most children died of starvation, disease, animal attacks, violence, and storms. Fortunate was the person who lived to adulthood.

Eventually, only one community remained. Some who lived there were desperate. Many had lost even their desperation as they patiently waited for death.

-from The Origin of Wild Magic *by Edoren the Bard*

"I want Orsen!" The cry rose from a hoarse throat and exited through lips pulled back over crooked teeth.

"Oh, Mama, I'm sorry." Kari took her mother's hand and immediately regretted it when her mother squeezed hard enough to bruise her fingers. Wincing, Kari said, "You're doing a good job."

From her seated position on her old, straw-filled mattress, Kari's mother threw off her daughter's hand and returned to her hands and knees, her animal grunt filling the room.

"I can see the head, Mama!" Kari pushed hard on her mother's back, just above the swell of her hips, where it always hurt during labor. "You're almost there!"

She was overstating it, and she knew it. This entire labor had been slow, and her mother's pushing was no exception. Only after two more hours did her mother's excruciating efforts at last pay off.

"Another girl!" Kari cried, helping her mother recline on lumpy pillows and placing the wailing babe in her shaking arms.

"A girl," her mother breathed. "Oh, Orsen loves his daughters. Maybe he'll come home and meet her." Her hopeful gaze fell on Kari's face.

"Maybe he will, Mama." Kari avoided her mother's eyes. She didn't believe it for a minute. Her papa had walked away half a year earlier with no farewell, tired of caring for a perpetually pregnant wife and nine children. He certainly wasn't coming back to meet the tenth.

Kari's mother spoke soft, adoring words to her screaming babe. She brought the child to her breast, and the crying stopped.

Before long, she pushed out the afterbirth. Kari placed it in a bowl and set to work tying the cord so she could cut it.

"Ohh."

Kari turned to her mother to see why she'd made that soft, moaning sound. Her mother's face was pale, eyes half-closed, arms limp under her new child.

"Mama, what's wrong?"

There was no answer.

Kari looked down to where the baby had emerged minutes before. She stumbled back, shocked by the quantity of thick, crimson blood spreading on the old birthing quilt underneath her mother's hips.

"Mama?" Kari grabbed her mother's shoulder and shook it hard. But her mother's eyes were blank. "Mama!"

The second "Mama" was a scream, and moments later, the bedroom door swung open.

"What's wrong?" Jenki asked, her eyes wide.

Kari was crying too hard to answer her little sister.

Jenki was thirteen, two years younger than Kari, and she'd helped with a couple of their mother's births. She ran up to the bed. "Mama!" she cried. She grabbed the baby, who was no longer suckling, and pushed the newborn's little mouth back onto their mother's breast. "It'll help the bleeding stop; Mama told me that!"

Kari couldn't move. She watched the baby latch onto a breast that wasn't moving up and down as it should be. Her mother's eyes were still partially open, as was her mouth, but she wasn't looking at anything.

Jenki looked up to the ceiling. "Sava!" she screamed. "Make my mama breathe!"

Kari stifled a sudden, humorless laugh. Jenki really thought the mysterious god in the sky would help their mother? They all heard stories of magic entering the world and helping people who were in trouble. But not people like them. If Sava existed, he certainly wasn't aware of the big family crammed into this dirty little house.

Jenki's gaze at last dropped from the silent ceiling and returned, hopeless, to their mother.

Kari walked toward the door, barely feeling the dirt floor under her bare feet.

"Where are you going?" Jenki asked.

Kari didn't turn as she answered, "To find a wet nurse."

"I CAN COME TWICE A DAY. You'll have to supplement with cow milk or goat milk the rest of the time."

Kari stared at the woman who lived three houses down. She was standing at her open door, bouncing her own baby on her hips.

"Did you hear me, Kari?"

Kari nodded.

"It'll be up to you to keep that baby fed. Twice a day from my breasts won't cover it. You'll have to be the one to mother that baby now. You'll have to mother all of them."

The woman's stern expression softened, and she stopped bouncing and placed a hand on Kari's shoulder. "I'm sorry about your mama. I really am. I've got a jar of goat milk from this morning. Give the baby a little bit now, and again at dusk. She's a wee one; she won't want much. I'll stop by tonight. Sava knows I've got plenty of extra milk; she can drink her fill."

Kari nodded, took the milk, and walked home.

KARI DIDN'T EXACTLY DECIDE to leave. She just woke in the middle of the night, two days after her mother's death and her sister's birth, and knew she had to go.

She was fifteen. She couldn't raise nine brothers and sisters. If she stayed, the whole town would expect her to take on her mother's responsibilities. Not just caring for her siblings, but the sewing that brought in barely enough income to keep their family alive. Kari was a terrible seamstress, but they'd still expect her to do it.

On her watch, her siblings would be shoeless and hungry. She knew it like she knew her own name. First, she'd watch them suffer, and then she'd watch them die—the little ones first, then the bigger ones, withering to nothingness, bellies protruding from starvation, finally drifting to sleep and not waking up. And all because their sister couldn't care for them.

If she left, surely the other families in the community would take her siblings in. They'd have to. Jenki was too young to care for the little ones; no one would expect that of a thirteen-year-old.

I don't want to go. But the alternative, letting her brothers and sisters suffer under her care when she was still a child herself, was unthinkable. *This is the only choice.*

Kari packed a bag and got dressed. She tiptoed to her mother's bed, then kissed her hand and held it over the three sleeping children there. She repeated the action at the doorway of the other tiny bedroom and at the entrance to the kitchen, where three children slept on the floor. By the time she held out her kissed fingers to the baby, who was wrapped in a blanket in an old basket near the stove, her hand was trembling uncontrollably.

She grabbed her mother's boots from their spot by the front door and fled outside, not stopping to put them on until she was two houses down. Then she walked toward the edge of town, gaze straight ahead, quiet tears washing her cheeks.

THE NEAREST CITY, Esherin, was a two-day walk from Kari's town.

The trip was miserable. Not the weather; it was sunny and warm. Kari had enough food, too, and she could refill her water skin in the nearby river as often as she needed to. She even found a barn with a comfortable hayloft to sleep in.

No, she wasn't experiencing physical discomfort. It was the silence that tortured Kari. It gave her time to think about her mama's last moments, to question what she could have done to stop the hemorrhage. Had she pulled on the cord, detaching the afterbirth before it was ready? She didn't think so, but perhaps she wasn't remembering clearly. What about herbs? Surely her mother had something that could have stopped the bleeding. Why hadn't Kari ever thought to ask that?

Every time she convinced herself to stop thinking along such lines, Kari instead questioned if she should have left. It was a terrible thing, sneaking out in the middle of the night. Her siblings would panic when they couldn't find her. She even thought of going back, but that wouldn't solve anything. Caring for nine siblings was impossible. She was fifteen, for Sava's sake.

But it didn't matter how many times she pictured her siblings safe and warm in the homes of benevolent townspeople. Another image kept intruding—her father leaving his family, just as she'd done.

I am a coward. A selfish coward.

She kept walking, the word *coward* echoing in her mind with every footstep.

When she reached the city, the odors of close living assaulted her—

open sewers, fresh bread, spices, unwashed bodies. She breathed it all in, begging the pungent scents to replace her torturous thoughts.

As she'd traveled, a question had occasionally interrupted her self-loathing: *Where will I stay in the city? What will I do?* She'd pushed such practical concerns away, convinced she'd find a job of some sort, assuring herself that once she made a little money in the city, she could even bring her siblings to live with her there.

But as she walked the unfamiliar streets of Esherin, her optimism fled. Nobody knew her here. What would they think of a stranger with no skills to speak of?

Kari gritted her teeth against her doubts. *Just go in the inn right there and ask for a job. It's not that hard.*

The inn had nice paint, flower boxes on the windowsills, and a big front porch where a woman was knitting. It looked like a place Kari's mother would approve of.

"Good afternoon," Kari said. "Are you the owner?"

The woman looked up. Her gaze flicked up and down Kari's form, and she grimaced. "No."

Kari glanced at her dusty dress and shoes. She looked like a traveler. *That's because I am a traveler. A confident traveler.* She lifted her chin. "Is the owner inside?"

"Yes." The woman returned her attention to her knitting.

Inside, Kari knocked on the open door of a small office. "Pardon me," she said to a short man with a thin face, "I'm looking for work. I can clean and even cook a little."

The owner appraised her with eyes even sterner than the woman's had been. "We have all the help we need." He stood and closed the door.

Well, then. Kari pressed her lips together and walked back outside.

As she made her way down the street, the establishments diminished in quality. But none of the inns, pubs, or taverns, even the seediest ones, were hiring.

By the time Kari reached the end of the street, she wasn't only dusty, she was sweaty. And she was holding back tears.

There was one more building. And this one looked nicer than

almost any of the others. It was two stories tall, with pale-pink siding, the trim bright white. There was no sign saying what type of establishment it was, but it had several hitching posts out front and on the side. Surely it was a business, not a residence.

She climbed the steps to the front porch and spotted someone there, squatting down, repairing the railing. His back was to her.

"Pardon me," Kari said in a voice that had grown quieter the farther she'd moved down the road.

The repairman turned around, and it turned out he wasn't quite a man at all. He must've been about her age. Behind the thick, dark-brown hair hanging on his forehead, his eyebrows lifted. "Do you need something?" he asked in the kindest voice she'd heard all day.

"I—I'm trying to find a job." Kari realized she was wringing her hands, and she forced them to her sides. "What is this place?"

The young man stood. He opened his mouth, closed it, swallowed, and opened it again. "Uh . . ." he said.

Kari stared at him, wondering if he was capable of conversation. When the silence lingered, she tried again. "Is there someone inside I could talk to?"

That loosed his tongue. "No!" Seeing her startle, he held his hands up and let out an awkward laugh. "Sorry. Miss . . . ?"

"Kari."

"Kari. I'm Havadom. You can call me Dom."

He held out his hand, and Kari shook it.

"Like I said, I'm looking for a job. Do you know if they're hiring here?"

"Listen, Kari, you don't want a job here. There are all sorts of pubs and inns on this street. Maybe one of them needs someone to serve or wash dishes."

"I've stopped at every single one." To Kari's horror, a lump filled her throat. She spoke past it. "Nobody is hiring, and I need work now."

He shook his head. "Not here. There are other places around town you can go to."

"Why not here?" Kari gestured toward the front door, which was glossy black and looked like it had been painted yesterday. "What's wrong with this place?"

"It's a brothel!" Then, like he'd just realized how loud he was, Dom looked around nervously. When he spoke again, his voice was hushed. "It's a brothel, Kari," he repeated. "You don't want to work here."

She stared at him, not answering because she didn't want him to hear her choked voice. When tears filled her eyes, she looked down to hide them. But one of them shoved its way out, streaking down her cheek. She wiped it away. He was right; she couldn't work at a brothel. But where else could she go?

Dom took a step closer to her. "Oh no, I'm sorry. Don't cry. You'll find work somewhere."

She nodded and turned to walk down the porch steps.

"Wait!" Dom called.

Kari turned.

"Can I do anything to help?"

"Not unless you can give me a job."

He opened his mouth, then shut it, looking helpless.

"I wasn't serious," Kari said, forcing a smile to her lips. "Thanks, but there's nothing you can do."

She spent the rest of the day walking through the city. She'd always heard it was a big place, but now that she was looking for work, it seemed surprisingly small. All the businesses were clustered along several streets. She made it to a few more of them before it got too late.

One of the inn owners took pity on her and gave her some stew for dinner. But other than that small comfort, Kari found only distrust and coldness. Either they weren't hiring, or, more likely, they'd only hire from locals who weren't grimy, sweaty, and unknown.

She slept fitfully in a garden in front of a big house. The next morning, she rose early to avoid being caught, then walked through town again.

Three days later, Kari had visited every place of business she could find, some of them twice. She didn't have one promising job prospect.

As the sun dipped low in the sky, she sat next to the sewer trench behind an inn, thinking back on the person she'd been when she'd arrived in the city, her belly full of traveling food, her dress a little dusty. That girl hadn't had an inkling what true desperation was. The state she was in now—starving, thirsty, hair matted where she'd slept on it, stinky enough to offend even herself—this was desperation.

Kari walked back to the pretty, pink house and knocked on the door.

"You can't let her stay here!"

Kari recognized that voice. It was Dom. He must be right outside the door of the parlor where she was waiting.

The response was muffled, and the conversation continued, Dom's voice occasionally increasing in volume. Then the door opened, and Dom rushed in, followed by the young woman who'd let Kari in.

"Kari, you can't stay here!" he said. "How old are you, anyway, sixteen? You can't do this!"

"Yes, I'm sixteen." The statement wouldn't be true for another half-year.

"Dom, you're not even supposed to be in the parlor!" the young woman said, tugging on his arm. "You'll get me in trouble!"

Dom ignored her words, pulling away and running up to Kari. He grasped her shoulders. "Kari, please, go home. Things can't be as bad there as they are here."

Kari couldn't tell this boy the truth—that she didn't have a home, and it was because she'd abandoned her family. He'd look at her with horror and disgust, and she couldn't bear that from one of the few people in the city who'd been kind to her.

"I'm staying," she said.

Dom's face fell, as did the volume of his voice. "If you stay here, the madam won't let you leave. Not until you're too old to bring her any business, and then you'll be worse off than you are now. Please, Kari. Go home. You'll find a job; just give it time."

But Kari couldn't think about what she'd do in a few decades when she was too old to work at this place. She had to take care of herself, and that couldn't wait. As much as she'd like a normal life, she'd ruined all chances of that when she'd left her family.

"Dom, you need to go." The young woman pulled at his arm again.

"Kari?" His eyes held hers, and they were full of a kind, passionate plea.

Kari looked away. "You do need to go. I'm staying here."

CHAPTER TWO

There lived in this community a sister and brother, as wretched and hopeless as their neighbors. Their names were Alena and Alaya.

On a day like any other, these two children went into the trees, seeking wood for their fire and food to cook on it. Their family had not eaten in six days, and the siblings were weak and cold from starvation.

"Perhaps," Alena told her brother, "we will find a squirrel."

"And perhaps," Alaya returned, "we should leave the squirrels alone and give in to death."

-from The Origin of Wild Magic *by Edoren the Bard*

"Get her in the tub."

Those were the only words Roza, the madam of Esherin House, spoke when she met Kari.

The young woman who'd brought Kari into the parlor said, "Yes,

Madam," before grasping Kari's elbow and ushering her through the first floor and out the back door.

"We take baths in the kitchen behind the house," she said, walking toward a large outbuilding that beckoned Kari with delicious smells.

"What's your name?" Kari asked just before they went inside.

The young woman's face broke into a smile. "Mara."

Mara opened the door, and a rush of warmth from the cookstove met Kari.

"We already ate dinner," Mara said. "We always eat early so we can get to work. There's some leftover stew if you want it." She looked at Kari, whose face had slackened with hungry desire. "Oh, dear, you do want some, don't you? You eat, and I'll fetch water for the tub. We've got a well out back." She picked up a bucket and walked out the kitchen's back door.

Kari found a bowl on a shelf and filled it from a pot on the stove. The stew wasn't very hot, but it was the best food she'd ever tasted. She ate slowly, afraid of upsetting her empty stomach. When she finished, Mara had two big pots of water heating on the stove and was working on a third.

At last, the water boiled, and Mara added it to a metal tub she'd already partially filled with cool water. "Hop on in," she said.

Kari froze. Was she expected to undress in front of this woman she'd just met?

Mara gestured to the tub. "It's ready!" She turned back to Kari, and her cheerful expression shifted to a troubled one. She placed a hand on Kari's dirty cheek. "Oh, sweetheart, you can't be modest in this place."

She turned away, but not fast enough to hide the pity in her eyes.

Kari slowly peeled off her clothes and stepped in the tub. Mara brought her soap. She didn't stare at Kari, but neither did she try to look away. "Your hair is nice," she said with a smile. "What do you call that, auburn? It'll stand out." Her hand came up to her own hair, which was glossy and black.

Kari had never thought much about her appearance. As she washed, she evaluated her body like she'd never seen it before. She was pretty enough, she supposed, with nice proportions and soft curves.

And she was in a place where men she didn't know would take pleasure in looking at her and touching her, their hands and eyes uninvited.

Kari had never even been kissed by a man, other than her father's gruff kisses to her forehead. *Oh, Sava, what was I thinking?* She began to cry.

Mara knelt next to the tub, her eyes wide. "Sweetheart, you can't cry. I know you want to; sometimes even I still want to, and I've been here five years. But you can't. If I know Roza, she'll be here soon, and she'll slap the tears out of you."

Mara stood and went to the window that faced the pink house. "She's coming now! Dry those eyes, Kari!"

Kari's nerves were suddenly stronger than her grief. She wiped her cheeks and swallowed her final sob just before the door swung open.

Roza entered. She was tall and looked like she'd once been beautiful. Now, however, her carefully coiffed, graying hair and expensive clothes couldn't compensate for the dour cruelty of her face. She stood over the tub with her arms crossed, and her eyes examined every part of Kari's body with the detachment of a woman picking out meat at a butcher.

Kari wanted to cover her breasts and the area between her legs, but something told her this would anger Roza. So she washed her hair and tried to ignore the woman's exacting gaze.

When Kari had rinsed the soap out of her hair, Roza at last spoke. "You'll do." She turned to Mara. "We've only got one room left. Show her to it. Tell her what she needs to know. She starts tomorrow, and you know how these young ones are."

Roza knelt next to the tub then, bringing her face close enough that Kari could have traced the frown lines between the madam's eyebrows. "My girls belong to me," Roza said. "I'll keep you fed and clothed, and I'll pay you. But you belong to me. Don't ever try to leave. I will send my husband to find you, and you'll regret even thinking you could get away."

She spoke the simple words in a low voice devoid of emotion. Kari tried to control her breathing.

"Do you understand?" Roza asked.

Kari nodded.

Roza grabbed Kari's ear and twisted it painfully. "It's *yes, Madam.*"

Kari tried not to wince. "Yes, Madam."

Roza let go and left without another word.

Kari's first customer hurt her. She didn't think it was intentional, but neither did he seem to notice. The pain, while unwelcome, came as no surprise. Mara had warned her it might hurt the first time.

But Kari hadn't anticipated the countless other sensations that engulfed her. She couldn't escape the smell of the man's sweat or ignore the callouses on his big hands. She knew she'd never forget his raspy laugh and the way his candlelit eyes devoured her.

For weeks, she was on edge, dreading the onset of evening, trying desperately to keep the fear and disgust off her face when men visited her. But after about two months, something shifted. She watched a man enter her room and felt only detachment. She relaxed her mouth into a smile, devoid of fear or warmth, a costume for her face.

Later, when her customers were gone and she was in bed alone, Kari reflected that spending time with men was simply something she must do, like brushing tangles out of her hair or cutting her toenails or scrubbing pots. She didn't like it, but for the first time that night, she had let her mind wander while the men did what they wanted, not returning her thoughts to the present until each client left.

Some nights it didn't work. Her body and soul begged to escape their slavery, and it was all she could do not to kick the men off her. But as time passed, those nights were fewer and further between, and Kari became more skilled at completing her distasteful tasks by rote, imagining she was anywhere but the tiny, windowless room on the second floor of Esherin House.

Roza didn't let the clients abuse the women of the house, at least not very badly. "You're my investments, and if a man devalues an investment, he cannot return," she said. Every room had a bell by the bed, and if it rang, Roza came. It didn't happen often, and Kari supposed she should feel thankful for that.

It wasn't the men who scared Kari the most; it was Roza and her husband Yolin. Kari dreaded opening her door and finding Yolin waiting. His pale skin, dark hair, and cold, blue eyes made frequent appearances in her nightmares. Yolin regularly visited all the women of the house but never paid for their services. When Kari had been there a few months, one of the women ran away. Yolin caught her and beat her, and then Roza locked her in a closet for a full week.

Kari was certain every woman wished she could flee. Roza was a taskmaster. She made her women service every single client, even on busy nights when Kari and the others were tired and sore. And despite Roza's promise to pay, Kari hadn't seen one coin. The madam claimed she was holding the money for safekeeping until Kari came of age. She never indicated how old "of age" was.

Several months into her new life, Kari was just going to sleep after a long night of work when her door opened.

"Can I come in?" Mara asked.

Kari sat up. "Of course." She and Mara often chose chatting over sleep.

Mara put her candle on the little table next to Kari's bell, sat on the bed, and got right to the point. "I'm pregnant."

Kari's eyes widened. "But the midwife gives us preventatives."

"They don't always work." Mara looked down at her hands. "And when they don't work, the midwife gives us tea to take care of it. That doesn't always work, either."

Kari cast her eyes on Mara's belly, but her loose gown camouflaged it.

Mara placed a hand under her breasts and another below her belly, flattening the fabric over a slight, round protrusion. "Roza said when the baby is almost here, I won't have to work. Between the end of my pregnancy and my recovery, I'll get at least two or three months off."

The relief on Mara's face brought tears to Kari's eyes. "And then what? How will you raise a baby here?"

Mara's expression went flat. "Roza will . . ." She swallowed and began again. "Roza will find a family who wants a baby. They'll . . . they'll compensate her for all my lost wages."

"She'll sell your baby?" Kari's voice was louder than she'd intended.

Mara stood, fists clenched. "Kari, I'll get months off work. I'm not thinking about what happens beyond that." She stormed out.

The next day, Mara was no longer angry. She complained to Kari that her back was already getting sore. On that day and throughout the pregnancy, Kari used the information she'd learned from her mother to give Mara tips on what to expect and how to deal with discomfort.

During these long months, Kari tried to focus on her role as Mara's caregiver rather than her distasteful evening tasks. In the routine of it all, her sixteenth birthday passed unnoticed.

When Mara at last went into labor, Roza said she'd wait to send for the midwife until the baby was almost there. The madam instructed Mara to labor on the floor to avoid staining the sheets.

Instead, Kari closed Mara's door and covered the bed in old blankets, insisting no woman should have to give birth on the floor. Then she helped Mara through her pains, just as she'd done for her mother so many times.

She'd never particularly liked helping her mother give birth, but it was different with a friend. For the first time since leaving home, Kari felt useful. *I could have been a midwife. And I would have been happy.* She shook her head at the thought. No sense dwelling on such impossibilities now.

In the end, Mara's labor progressed more quickly than expected. With the midwife still en route, Kari guided the baby out of Mara's body.

As soon as Kari said, "It's a girl," Roza grabbed the child, not even allowing Mara to hold her daughter while Kari cut the cord. Mara cried all day and for weeks after. And then she went back to work.

After that, Kari noticed changes in her friend. Mara belittled clients who failed to show her respect, sometimes driving them away entirely. And she perfected her mask of adoration, reserving it for the kindest men, earning their loyalty. Kari admired Mara's ability to take some control of her life, a victory most of her housemates found impossible to achieve.

Having seen Kari's relative expertise with pregnancy and birth, another woman of the house soon confided that she was expecting. This time, the midwife's tea worked, and Kari attended her friend through a painful miscarriage, crying along with her. Afterward, Kari took to her own room, exhausted, yet once again feeling unexpectedly useful.

As her seventeenth birthday approached, Kari assisted two more of her housemates through their brief pregnancies and heartbreaking losses. It seemed the midwife's preventatives were less effective than she claimed—but her tea usually took care of "the problem," repeatedly introducing heartbreak into the brothel.

One of the women bled heavily during her miscarriage. Images of Kari's mother filled her mind—lying in blood, eyes glazed—and she was sure her new friend would have the same result. The young woman embraced the possibility, begging Sava to take her. But her body was too young and strong, and Sava, Kari thought, couldn't spare even the magic of a quick death for the likes of them. A few weeks later, the woman was back to work, paler than before, eyes having lost their last bit of joy.

Mara and some of the other women began calling Kari their "in-home midwife." Even with months in between any such duties, and even with the inherent tragedy of such a role in this place, Kari embraced the title. She occasionally indulged in dreams that one day she'd be a real midwife, doing all she could to bring living children into the world. But every night, a never-ending stream of men reminded her that her true career wasn't anything so fulfilling.

In between clients, life was manageable, if not pleasant. It was impossible not to compare it to her old friends' lives back home. She could guess which of them would have jumped into early marriages and who would still be caring for siblings or parents. What would they think if they knew where Kari had ended up? What would her siblings think? She'd long ago released any hope of returning to them and could only pray they were cared for—and that they wouldn't find out where she was.

After the cold, hungry nights scattered through her childhood, Kari did appreciate the amenities at Esherin House. She had nice clothing and good food, though Roza limited their portions. "Men come here to get away from their fat wives," Roza said. Kari didn't think even Roza believed such nonsense; several clients regularly complained that the women of Esherin House all looked the same. "Why don't any of you have any meat on you?" one man always asked Kari. But food was one more way for the madam to control *her girls.*

The house itself was far nicer than the dirty little home Kari had grown up in. Roza often hired Dom to do repairs and improvements. He always treated the women kindly, looking in their eyes and not at their bodies, even refusing Roza's offers to "take your tips from the house merchandise."

When he came, Dom always seemed to find Kari. He was nice enough, but his eyes brimmed with concern for her. *I don't want or deserve your pity,* Kari wanted to say. She kept the thought to herself and usually found something else to do when he tried to trap her in conversation.

As time wore on, however, Kari found it harder to avoid him. Dom was so kind compared to the men who visited her at night. And while she'd convinced herself she was immune to attraction of any sort, she kept noticing that Dom had grown taller, his shoulders broader. His dark hair was usually shaggy, and there was something about the way it fell on his forehead. A few times, she had to stop herself from reaching up to brush it away from his eyes.

He turned seventeen about the same time she did, and he told her he'd finished school and was working hard so he could purchase his own home. Most of the establishments on the street used his services, just as the brothel did, and he had more work than he could handle.

He persisted in seeking out Kari, and at last, she indulged her desire for his friendship. They talked while Dom painted the porch, repaired the banister, or did any number of other tasks. He told her about his family and his work, and eventually, she reciprocated, sharing tales of her childhood.

After weeks of this, Kari told Dom about her mother's death. Then, for some reason she couldn't pinpoint, she confessed to abandoning her siblings. She could barely get the words through her tight, trembling throat, and she immediately regretted the disclosure. But Dom responded with pure compassion in his deep, brown eyes, almost too much for Kari to bear.

That same day, she began trusting him with tales of her life in the brothel. She described how much she dreaded visits from Mekel, a man who'd become one of her regulars.

"Does he hurt you?" Dom's whole body was still, and his eyes bored into Kari's.

"No, it's not that." Heat rushed into Kari's face, and she would have slapped herself for it if that wouldn't have made her even redder. In her line of work, embarrassment was plain silly.

Dom's gaze wouldn't leave her, so Kari explained, "He insults me the whole time we're together. He points out everything he hates about my body and my face. Even the way I talk." She laughed and hoped it didn't sound as counterfeit as it felt. "It's silly; I don't know why he keeps coming back if he's so unhappy with me."

Dom didn't say a word, but his jaw muscles tightened. He picked up his hammer and resumed his task repairing the front steps, hitting the nails harder than seemed necessary. When Kari rose to leave, he looked up at her. "Wait." His face relaxed into a warm smile. "I wanted to tell you about a traveler at one of the inns down the street."

Dom then told her a story that made her laugh harder than she had in months. When he finished, she sat on the porch and studied him, wondering why he was the only male in the city who seemed more interested in her company during the day than at night.

That evening, Kari paced in her room, door cracked open, wondering who'd visit her first. She heard the front door open, and the voice that reached her ears made her stop in her tracks. It was Dom. *He never works here at night.*

Most of Dom's words weren't audible from Kari's room, but one stood out: *tips.*

Every word of Roza's loud response floated upstairs. "It's about time!" She laughed, a high-pitched, piercing sound. "Go on up."

Kari sat on the edge of her bed, her entire body tense. Dom was at last taking the *tips* Roza had often offered him. *Whose room will he visit? Whose room do I want him to visit?*

She recoiled at the thought of Dom with any of the other women of the house. And yet she didn't want him to come to her, either. He'd always treated her as an equal. The first step he took through her door as a client would forever mark him as one more man proving his power over her.

But oh, dear Sava, the last thing in the world Kari wanted was to hear one of her friends giggling the next day about an unexpected tryst with Dom.

Footsteps sounded on the stairs.

Just turn around, Kari begged silently. *Just go. This isn't you, Dom. You're not like all those other men.*

The steps continued. All the way into Kari's room.

As soon as she saw him, she swallowed, pushing back tears. "Hello, Dom."

He closed the door and stood in front of her. Kari met his gaze but couldn't hold it. Her eyes dropped to his dirty boots.

"Kari." He cleared his throat. "I saw Mekel headed this way, so I ran ahead of him."

She blinked. He'd come here to rescue her from her least-favorite client? It was a kind thing to do, but how could she tell him she dreaded his touch more than Mekel's?

Dom knelt so his head was lower than Kari's. From her position on the edge of the bed, she kept her eyes on his feet.

"Can—can you look at me, Kari?"

"You're a client." She shoved the words through her tight throat. "The only right answer is yes." Dreading the hot demands of his gaze, Kari clenched her teeth and looked up.

What Kari found in Dom's eyes caused her jaw to drop and lips to part. Tenderness waited on every gentle aspect of his face.

"I thought if I came in here, you could escape Mekel, at least tonight. But—" Dom looked away for a moment, then met her gaze again. "I'm not here as a client, Kari. I'm here as a friend. I thought maybe we could just . . . you know . . . talk. Like we always do. How long do you think I can get away with staying here?"

Tears returned to Kari's eyes, but they were tears of gratitude and relief, not dread. "Roza will knock on the door once you've been here too long."

Dom smiled. "Great. I'll stay until then."

Kari sniffled and returned the smile. "I'd offer you a chair, but there aren't any." She scooted over. "Have a seat?"

Dom sat next to her on the bed but didn't look at her. "Kari, when I first met you, if I'd known you didn't have a home, I would have asked you to come stay with my family." He glanced at her, then looked down at his hands, which were folded tightly on his lap. "I wish I'd asked you where you lived. I don't know why I didn't."

Kari opened her mouth, but it was too dry. She licked her lips and swallowed, then croaked, "You would have asked me to stay with your family? You didn't know me."

His eyes found hers, and this time, they didn't stray away. "My parents always help people if they need it. I just wish I'd known, Kari." He leaned toward her, his face uncomfortably close to hers. She flinched, and he drew back, but his gaze didn't lose any of its intensity. "You could still leave. Come to my house. Tonight."

Kari pulled her eyes away, looking at the door. "This is my life now, Dom. Pub owners wouldn't hire me when I first got here, just because they didn't know me. They wouldn't even let me across their thresholds now. Besides, if I left, Yolin would find me. He . . . he doesn't treat women well when they run away."

"My father is the head safety officer. We'd protect you. My parents and I would try to find some sort of job for you."

"Oh, Dom." Kari brought a hand up to her cheek and wiped away a tear. Dom's promises were full of idealism, but he had no idea what it would really be like to be on the run from Yolin, who didn't care a whit who the head safety officer was. It would be impossible to find even a menial job in a hostile town full of men who visited her in private but would shun her in public. She took a shaky breath. "It's too late to change who I am."

She heard Dom's deep sigh before he said, "I live in the blue house on the street behind this one. You can't miss it. If you ever decide you're done with all this, please come to my house. We'll help you. I promise."

Kari didn't know how to answer. Part of her wanted to run out the front door with Dom right then. But people knew who she was. She knew who she was. There was no way to change that.

After an awkward silence, their conversation resumed. At first, it was stilted. But after a few minutes, they were sharing stories and laughing like they did when Dom painted the porch railing or repaired a windowsill. True to his word, he stayed until Roza kicked him out. As he left, he caught her eye and whispered, "Blue house."

The next day, Mara told Kari that Mekel had visited her. She'd thrown his insults right back at him, offending him so deeply, he'd promised never to return. Roza was furious, but Mara brought in more business than any of the other women. The madam wouldn't punish her top income source for driving away one client.

From then on, as often as Roza allowed, Dom visited Kari. When the other residents of the house teased them both, they smiled, enjoying their shared secret—that Dom was the one man who visited Kari's room and never touched her.

Days in the brothel passed quickly, nights slowly. And seasons shifted at the pace they always had, time seeming meaningless in this place where not much ever varied except the men visiting Kari at night.

A couple of months before her eighteenth birthday, Kari looked at the slip of paper where she kept track of the passing days, weeks, and months, and she realized six weeks had gone by since she'd last bled. Her first reaction was annoyance. Roza gave them time off during their bleeding days, and she was ready for a break.

But that annoyance quickly hardened into a knot of fear in her gut. And she suddenly realized that same gut had felt sick more often than usual for the last few days.

Another week passed, then another. She knew she should tell Roza, who would bring her to the midwife for doses of the dreaded tea. But try as she might, Kari couldn't think of the child growing inside her as a problem to be fixed. *Mama was younger than this when she had me.*

Her life, she knew, was incompatible with motherhood. Even if she were allowed to care for her child, she'd never know which of a score of different men was the father.

Despite all this, Kari couldn't release her irrational desire to not only give birth to her baby, but also to nurture it. Sava help her, she wanted to be a mother.

Her nausea wasn't severe. She hadn't even vomited once. She knew how lucky she was; vomiting in the brothel earned a woman an immediate visit from the midwife. And no one seemed to have noticed she'd never taken her days off that month.

Kari treasured her secret. Late each night when she had her bed to herself, she covered her still-flat belly with a warm hand, sending love to the child within her.

But then the flatness turned slightly round, and Kari knew it wouldn't be long before Roza's sharp eyes noticed the difference. Already, she'd seen the madam staring at her chest, which these days threatened to burst out of her low-cut dresses.

Kari visited Mara late one night, just as Mara had done to her two years earlier.

"Where did they take your baby?" Kari asked.

Mara blinked tiredness from her eyes. "It's late. I don't want to talk about that."

"Please." Kari's voice cracked. "Where did they take your daughter, Mara?"

Mara tilted her pretty head to the side and looked down at Kari's body. Her eyes came up to Kari's face, and it must have been there that she found the truth, because she began to cry as she reached out and held her friend. "Oh no, not you, too. I'm so sorry."

Kari returned the embrace but didn't indulge in tears. She couldn't afford anything but strength right now. When Mara let go of her and sat back, Kari took the hands of the woman she considered her sister. "I want you to know," she said, "you are a kind, generous person. A *good* person, Mara. So good."

They were the words Kari wished someone would say to her, wished she were worthy of.

But Mara didn't respond with gratitude. Her brows drew together, and she shook her head. "Kari, don't run away."

Kari gaped at her friend. How did she know?

"Don't!"

The word was harsh and almost compelled Kari to reconsider. Almost.

"Goodbye, Mara."

Kari returned to her room, got dressed, crept downstairs, opened the front door, and walked to the road. Fleeing, it turned out, was easy.

Until she was halfway down the street and heard the running footsteps behind her.

CHAPTER THREE

They found one squirrel, then another, but the animals were too fast for the children, whose hunger had stolen their quickness. As dusk set in, Alena and Alaya turned toward home, barely strong enough to carry the sticks they had gathered.

Just as they left the trees, a mighty sound emerged from the forest behind them, a roar unlike any they had heard before.

-from The Origin of Wild Magic *by Edoren the Bard*

KARI LOOKED BEHIND HER, an action she immediately realized was pointless. The street was dark except for a little light shed by the stars and a full moon.

But she didn't need light to know who was running after her. It was Roza's husband Yolin, the last person she wanted to encounter on any street, during the day or at night.

The street was muddy, thanks to a recent autumn shower. The only shoes Kari had were slippers with felt soles and velvet uppers, designed to look lovely and feminine. And, Kari now realized, also designed to keep the wearer indoors. The felt squished in the mud, providing little traction. The mud and darkness hid uncountable little rocks, and every time her foot came down on one, it hurt.

But none of that mattered. She had to get away. While Roza didn't let men abuse the women of Esherin House, she made an exception for Yolin when a prostitute fled. Kari had even heard Roza giving him instructions when he'd captured a runway: "She needs to heal within a week, at least well enough to look good in the dark and be able to do her duties!"

Faster, faster, faster! The internal chant matched her panicked steps.

"Kari!" Yolin shouted, his voice echoing off the quiet buildings. He panted as he called, "I just . . . want to bring . . . you home! . . . No punishment!"

She didn't believe that for a second. *Faster!*

Her slipper came down on an extra-slick patch of mud, and Kari fell hard, barely getting her hands underneath her in time to break her fall. Her wrists would ache the next day. She'd protected her baby, though. That was all that mattered.

In an instant, she was up, but Yolin's footsteps were closer. She ran again, this time weighed down by her wet, muddy dress. Sobs threatened to emerge from her chest, but she refused them. She couldn't spare the air.

"Kari, stop!" Yolin's voice was so close. Too close.

He wasn't that strong, but it didn't take much physical fitness to run faster than a woman who stayed inside all day, every day. Yolin, on the other hand, often took long walks. Kari had seen him strolling down the street while she sat at a window, wishing she could leave too.

The realization hit her all at once in between two gasping breaths: *I can't outrun him.*

At that moment, a cloud covered the moon. Kari's open mouth widened into a feral grin. Hoping the additional darkness was enough to blind Yolin and that her ridiculous shoes were quiet, she put on another burst of speed. The strength came, she was convinced, from the child within her. She moved off the road, running all the way to an inn on her left.

Kari slowed to pick up two palm-sized rocks that bordered a path leading to the inn. She flung the rocks ahead, to the other side of the street, then hunched down, making herself as small as she could against the building's face.

It was too dark to see Yolin, but she heard him pass her as he panted, "Did you . . . fall again? . . . Let . . . me help."

It worked! Yolin thought the rocks were the sound of her falling.

She hadn't regained her breath, but she knew the ruse wouldn't last long. She had to keep moving.

Kari stood again and sprinted around the inn, running to its rear. There was a narrow passage back there with an open sewer all the businesses used. She ran close to the buildings, trying to avoid the foul-smelling trench. She headed back the direction she'd come, increasing the distance between her and Yolin.

Her right foot slipped, landing hard in the malodorous muck of the sewer trench. Her ankle twisted with a sickening *pop*.

No, no, no! Kari pulled her foot out of the goo and ran another couple of steps. But her ankle couldn't hold her. She fell again, this time on her backside, the edges of her vision turning blacker than the sky.

She tried to stand, but the pain was too great. Dropping to her knees, she vomited onto her dress.

I didn't even aim for the sewer. Why didn't I aim for the sewer?

She hadn't fled with a plan beyond *get away*. Escaping had been a far-fetched idea, even with two functional feet. Now, it was impossible.

No, not impossible! She wouldn't give up, not until Yolin's meaty hands grasped her. *Not even then.*

Kari began to crawl. Even that was painful, her ankle throbbing with every movement. She gritted her teeth and kept going.

Right hand and knee. Left hand and knee. Right hand and knee—

"Kari?" Yolin's voice came from behind the buildings. His breaths and footsteps were still rapid. "You back here?"

No! Kari's grieved cry was silent, but it resonated in her chest. She kept crawling, despite the uselessness of the effort.

"Sava!" Kari whispered, her voice no more than a pained breath. She knew her prayer was as pointless as her crawl, but she had no other options. "Help!"

Warmth flooded her ankle, and Kari almost sobbed, mistaking it for pain. But no, this didn't hurt, not even a little. This felt good, like a blanket heated before a fire, wrapped tight around her injured joint. And as the warmth increased, the pain fled.

Holding her breath, Kari slowly shifted herself off her hands and knees and onto her feet. In a squat now, she gradually moved some of her weight onto the foot she'd just injured.

The pain was gone. Her ankle was healed.

Energy renewed, Kari ran. She didn't stop until she was in the woods outside town, having left Yolin's panting cries behind her several minutes before.

She fell again to her knees, this time in gratitude, rather than desperation.

"Thank you," she said, the words chopped apart by a sob.

KARI SLEPT in a pile of dry leaves. She shouldn't have been able to sleep at all. Autumn was nearly over, and temperatures were dropping.

But she wasn't cold. She woke with the sun, and she knew her warm limbs and healed ankle were the result of magic.

Magic—for me. She'd never even dared to dream of such a thing.

Was this help truly a gift from Sava, a god people knew little about? No one could predict when magic would enter the world or who it would touch when it did. Sometimes, someone received unexplainable assistance when they were in trouble. After that first touch, magic might never come to them again, or it might follow them for a time, like a benevolent spirit.

Perhaps Sava was the father of magic. It was harder to believe such things in the light of day than it had been in the terrifying darkness the previous night. Whatever the source, Kari was grateful.

She lay her hand, still warm from the night's supernatural heat, on the gentle curve of her belly. "Hello," she said, her voice soft. It was the first time she'd dared talk to the growing child inside her. "I don't know how we're going to survive out here, but I'll do whatever I can to protect you."

Her hand vibrated—not with the movement of the baby; it was too early for that. No, this trembling came with an audible growl. She needed food and water.

Kari stood, stretched, and began to walk. The magical warmth was gone now, but the sun was bright, making the autumn air bearable. She had been walking for several minutes when she realized her foot, the one that had healed the night before, wasn't heavy with dried sewage. She looked down, then immediately sat, grabbing her foot between both hands.

Her shoe was clean. It looked brand new, and the stocking underneath appeared freshly laundered. And Kari didn't know why she hadn't noticed it before, but her dress, too, was pristine. It was the coppery brown of finely dyed fabric, not the brown of the mud she'd fallen in the day before. There was no trace of her vomit, either.

That wasn't all. Despite walking on the rough forest floor, her feet didn't hurt. She took off a shoe and examined the sole. It was still made of felt, but it was thicker and more durable than it had been before.

Kari allowed herself a smile. Magic had indeed come to visit her. It probably wouldn't stay, but she only had to look at her shoes to prove to herself it had been real. She looked up, and her smile turned into a peal of laughter. Right next to her on the little game path she'd been exploring was a blueberry bush, full of ripe fruit, though it wasn't blueberry season. She filled her empty stomach with the berries. They were perfect, juicy and sweet with just a hint of tartness. Then she pulled the hem of her skirt up and tied it tight around her waist. She placed more berries in the resulting pouch, leaving only her slip and pantalettes to keep her legs warm.

When she'd finished picking most of the fruit off the bush, she closed her eyes and sat, listening to the woods.

Water. Bubbling and fresh.

She followed the sound and found a pristine creek where she slaked her thirst. These woods seemed to be welcoming her. But Kari knew she couldn't stay. Yolin was too close. She sat under a tree, considering where to go next.

She could go to Dom's. But as quickly as the thought arose, she dismissed it. He lived too close to the brothel. No matter how good of a safety officer Dom's father was, he couldn't protect her day in and day out. Roza and Yolin would find her, and when the time came, they would take her baby.

Home beckoned, but she certainly hadn't gained any useful skills that would allow her to care for her siblings. And besides, her hometown was too close. People would find out the truth of her child's parentage. *I can't bring that shame on my family.*

Her only option was to flee to a city where no one knew her. She would pose as a widow. Surely someone would have mercy on her and give her an honest job.

Kari stood and took a deep breath, fortifying her courage. She began to walk, and a couple of hours later, she reached the far edge of the woods. Still shaded by the tall trees, she examined a broad meadow spread out before her. In the distance, she saw a few scattered homes. Surely there was a road past the houses, a path to a new future for her and her child.

She stepped out of the trees and into the meadow. Immediately, something felt different. She couldn't pinpoint what it was, but she kept going.

Kari had only taken a few steps when heard a distinct sound at her feet: *Sssss.* Her eyes snapped downward. A snake waited there, poised to strike.

A jolt of shock surged through each of her limbs. Before her senses could recover, her legs spun her around, propelling her into a sprint. She'd seen the orange mark between the creature's eyes. *Fire viper.* One bite from its long fangs would stop her heart in minutes.

As Kari ran, her heart pounded so hard, she feared it would kill her if the snake didn't. Her panicked strides dislodged the knot in her skirt, and her blueberries tumbled into the grass.

When she'd traveled far enough to convince herself she was safe, she slowed to a walk, caught her breath, and reoriented herself, determined to take the most direct path out of the meadow. This time, she kept her eyes down, alert for danger in the path.

A quarter of the way to the distant houses, another snake waited in Kari's path. Its body was coiled, and from either side of an orange blotch, intelligent black eyes watched her. It greeted her with an ominous hiss.

This time, Kari turned and fled back into the woods. For her to encounter two fire vipers in such a short time, the meadow must be full of them. She'd have to find another route out of the forest.

But as soon as she exited the meadow, a sense of serene safety fell on her. All at once, she identified what she'd felt upon leaving the trees earlier. It was the sudden absence of magic. She'd entered the normal world, where snakes and any number of other dangers waited. Now she was back under the forest's strange protection.

Over the coming days, Kari tried repeatedly to leave the woods. She had to get farther from Yolin. But each time, she encountered danger beyond the trees and safety within them. The message was clear: *This is where you're meant to be.* And so, despite her fear, she stayed.

Magic touched her in various practical ways. She stayed warm enough, even without a fire. Her diet consisted of out-of-season berries, which often seemed to grow overnight, along with mushrooms. At first, she expected to feel weak due to the lack of meat, but magical energy sustained her.

It wasn't an easy life. Sometimes she had to walk for hours to find food. When she had extra, she dried it, then buried it in leaf-lined holes so animals wouldn't steal it. Despite her experience the first day, her clothes did get dirty. She had to wash her full-length slip and pantalettes in the stream while she wore only her thin dress, and then she had to do the opposite once her slip was dry.

Even with these challenges, living in the forest felt right, more right than anything had since fleeing her home over two years before.

Yes, she was alone. She often dreamed about laughing with Mara or talking with Dom in her room. *But I don't need people,* she reminded herself. *And other people certainly don't need me.* She hadn't even had the presence of mind and forethought to save her mother. She'd left her siblings without saying goodbye. Something in her heart was evil enough to lead her to abandon the people who needed her the most.

Kari had nothing to offer the world except her body, but she'd die before returning to the brothel. She was constantly aware how undeserving she was of the child inside her, and despite knowing her own mother had started a family early, Kari felt anything but ready. It was strange how, after two years of being used by men, she still felt like a child herself.

But whether or not she was deserving or prepared, she'd do all she could to protect her baby, here in the forest, away from the evils of the world. She would prove to her child—and to herself—that she was capable of love.

Three weeks into her stay in the woods, Kari washed her dress again and laid it on a flat stone where she often dried blueberries. She stretched out on the hard ground next to the stone, soaking up the early winter sun. The dry leaves on the forest floor had been frosty that morning, but over the past week, as the weather had gotten colder, magical warmth had encompassed Kari not only at night, but also throughout the day. It was soothing, an invisible quilt of comfort. Today, she'd even taken her shoes and socks off, giving her tired feet a rest.

She was singing a soft lullaby to the child within her when she heard a voice. She could barely make out the words: "Good thing I wore my hat; it's cold under these trees."

Kari's eyes snapped open. She sat up, pulled her knees to her chest, and huddled behind the big rock. She was about to reach up and pull her dress out of sight when the same voice reached her ears.

"What's that? On the rock?"

Kari knew that scratchy, scornful voice. *Yolin.*

She held her breath. Maybe he'd walk off.

Who am I kidding? He saw my dress. He'd find her, and she'd better be running when he did.

Kari pushed herself to her feet, held her slip up, and sprinted away. Behind her, Yolin cried out, his rushed steps crunching against the dry leaves on the forest floor.

"Stop!" he yelled. "Let's go home, Kari! There's food at home!"

His pleas weren't any more effective than they'd been the day she fled the brothel. Kari continued to run.

But without her shoes, her bare feet felt every root and rock. Even the crisp stems of dead leaves stabbed her soft soles. Soon, every step was painful.

Yolin's distant voice reached her. "Where'd you go, Kari? Stop!"

He lost me! But even if Yolin couldn't see her through the trees, his voice was still too close. Kari's lungs and limbs were on fire, but she urged her legs to keep going, her feet to forget the pain.

She passed tree after tree, panic making it difficult to discern familiar landmarks. Her feet stumbled more times than she could count. Still she ran, though her pace slowed. Yolin didn't seem to get any closer nor any farther, always within earshot but never catching up.

After running for what felt like an hour, Kari's head felt light, her thoughts sluggish. Her anxious footsteps took her to the edge of the trees. A large, fallow field sat between the forest and Esherin.

I have to go to the city. Yolin wouldn't chase her through busy streets. Not in the middle of the day. She'd disappear among the throngs, find a place to hide, and return to the forest at night.

Kari's aching feet leapt onto the dry grass, so much smoother than the debris-filled forest floor. She ignored the odd jolt that rushed through her as she left the trees. The city was so close. She put on an extra burst of speed.

But she'd been running too long, and her body screamed for her to stop. Her sweaty hands lost their grip on her cotton slip. It fell, blocking her view of the ground. Her left foot came down on a sharp rock. She cried out, instinct driving her to lift that foot higher. When she brought it back down, her toes caught the edge of her slip, and she fell hard.

Yolin's celebratory cry reached Kari's ears as she hit the ground. Her own loud breathing had drowned out his footfalls in the grass, and she was horrified to hear how close his voice was.

No! She clambered to her hands and knees, but Yolin was too close. He tackled her, his weight centered on her upper back. Cheek pressed into the yellow grass, wind forced from her lungs, Kari's first thought was that at least he hadn't landed lower on her back. Hopefully her baby was safe.

A moment later, Yolin's hands were on her neck, and every thought but one fled: *Air!* She lifted her hands and grasped Yolin's thick fingers, but she couldn't pry them off. Even her nails digging into his skin didn't deter him.

Yolin loosened his hands just enough for Kari to wheeze in a thin breath. In her relief, she dropped her hands, forgetting her defense. Yolin pulled his hands off her throat just long enough to grab her arms, wrench them down, and pin them to the ground beneath his heavy knees. In a snap, his hands returned to her throat, tight enough to induce panic, loose enough to allow tiny gasps of air to pass through.

He brought his mouth down to her face, his hot breath invading her ear. "I'm not gonna kill you," he said, his voice like a knife on stone. "I'm gonna bring you home. Roza owns you. Your neck is gonna hurt tomorrow, but if you're real nice, I won't break any bones. Except maybe some of your toes. You don't need toes for your work." His perverse laugh filled the air.

Yolin's hands loosened further, and Kari finally had enough air to think clearly. *I have one chance.*

Pushing down with her arms—an easy task, considering they were already pinned to the ground—she used every bit of energy she could find to swing her head up.

It slammed against Yolin's nose. He grunted and released Kari's neck, his knees loosening enough for her to pull her arms free. She couldn't do much when she was on her stomach, but she swung her elbows back, striking Yolin's thighs and knees.

He grunted again, then lowered his head and cursed at her. Kari changed tactics, lifting her hands, trying to scratch any part of him she could find. The nails on her right hand found the coarse flesh of Yolin's face, and she felt his skin tear.

He cried out, and the weight on Kari lessened. With a roar, she pushed her body up, forcing his hips off her. She flipped onto her back. She could see Yolin's face now. Blood ran from his nose and the wound on his cheek, stark against his pale skin. His entire face, looming above her, was twisted with ire.

Yolin tried to sit on her again, but Kari had already drawn her fist back. She punched between his legs, the action propelled by her desperate anger. Her knuckles drove the rough fabric of Yolin's pants into his soft flesh underneath. Hands falling to his groin, he toppled sideways, striking the ground hard.

Kari scrambled to her feet and ran, but instead of heading to the city, she sprinted back to the forest. She'd felt the loss of magic as soon as she'd left; why hadn't she turned around then? Yolin had lost her in the forest; if she'd stopped running, perhaps magic would have continued to protect her from him.

She found a thick group of trees and huddled in their shadows, struggling to control her loud breathing. Her hand cradled her belly which, thank Sava, didn't feel injured.

After perhaps an hour of silence, Kari crept out of her hiding place and carefully walked back to her little campsite, next to the big rock. Every step on her bruised, cut feet hurt. There was no sign of Yolin, and Kari released a deep, relieved sigh. She was sore, but she was safe.

Her next breath, however, caught in her lungs, for the rock where she'd left her dress was empty.

Kari rushed to the rock, searching all around it. The garment hadn't fallen off. Yolin had taken it. But that wasn't the worst of it. He'd taken her shoes and stockings too.

So much for magical protection. I should have gone to the city. Why did I ever think I could survive in this place? Perhaps she'd angered her mysterious supernatural benefactor when she'd left the trees. Clearly she was no longer worth protecting.

Kari looked up to the sky, shaking both fists at the winter sun and the invisible source of magic who'd failed her. She'd never claimed to deserve the help, but she'd learned to depend on it. How was she supposed to care for a child without it? She released a ragged scream, which turned into a sob.

She'd actually started to feel safe in this place. But now her vulnerability screamed at her with every throb of her feet. Yolin would return, of that she was certain. The next time, he'd catch her.

It was almost dusk. Kari had to find a safe place to sleep. And if magic had left the forest, she would have to do the same.

CHAPTER FOUR

As one, Alena and Alaya turned their dirty faces toward the sound. They needed not look far, for at the edge of the trees loomed a great, black bear, her claws in the air, her mouth open as she again roared her evil intent.

-from The Origin of Wild Magic *by Edoren the Bard*

KARI SLEPT within the same tight grouping of trees she'd hidden in the day before. She woke in the morning, and her eyes widened. Light snow had fallen overnight, the first of the season. It rested lightly on tree boughs and sparkled on the brown leaves of the forest floor. But Kari, wearing only a thin slip, was warm and dry.

Magic is still protecting me. It was the last thing she'd expected. But after the theft of her shoes and dress, she was all too aware of magic's capriciousness. There would be more snow, and her protection could stop at any time. She had to find shelter.

Standing, Kari assessed her situation. Apparently the benevolent giver of magic couldn't spare any healing powers. Her neck was sore and bruised, the cuts on her bare feet angry and red. How was she to search for a new home if she could barely walk?

She took a tentative step, accompanied by a sharp intake of breath. It didn't matter what she stepped on today. It would hurt, regardless.

Kari put her hand on the swell of her abdomen, whispered, *Child, give me strength*, and walked toward her former campsite. She hated to go there; Yolin could be waiting. But she'd stored her dried berries in a hole there, and she needed to eat. She'd just have to be careful.

The walk was torturous and slow. Kari tried to place her feet carefully, but the thin layer of snow hid many rocks and roots. Several times, she cursed in pain or gave in to tears. At such a slow pace, the walk back to her campsite felt endless.

When she did arrive, the area was, thankfully, deserted. She went to the tree she'd buried her food under. Lifting the rock that covered the leaf-lined hole, she found the dried berries waiting. She ate her fill and dropped the rest into the bodice of her slip. It was tight enough around her waist these days to make an effective carrying pouch. That done, she walked slowly to the creek, where she took a drink and washed her aching feet.

It was time to get out of this place. Kari trod to the edge of the clearing. She turned to say a silent goodbye to the spot that had been her home for three weeks.

Something on the ground on the other side of the rock stuck out just enough to catch her eye. She squinted but couldn't tell what it was. Well, she certainly wasn't taking any unnecessary steps today. She turned and had barely begun to walk again when a voice murmured to her heart, *Go back*.

Kari jolted; the message had been inaudible yet utterly clear. She shook her head. Too much time alone in this forest.

Go back.

The voice was even clearer this time. Kari stopped and turned with an audible groan. She took one painful step after another, back to the rock.

Waiting for her on the snowy ground was a pair of boots, crafted of soft leather, with thick, sturdy soles.

The sight grew hazy as tears entered Kari's eyes. Her head snapped up, and she fully expected to see Yolin run out of the forest, gleeful that his bait had worked.

But she was still alone.

Tears now rolling down her warm cheeks, Kari picked up the boots and ran back into the forest, ignoring her pain. When she'd gone just far enough that the rock was out of sight, she stopped, brushed a thin layer of snow off the ground to expose the leaves underneath, and sat.

Inside the boots, she found two pairs of thick socks, a comb, and a clay jar. Kari pulled the stopper out of the jar. A thick, herbal scent greeted her—the smell of healing. She tipped the jar over, and ointment oozed onto her hand. After spreading it on her sore feet, she put on both pairs of socks, followed by the boots. They fit perfectly.

Boots, socks, a comb, and ointment? Kari mused over the items as she combed three weeks' worth of tangles from her hair. These were such concrete gifts to come from a spiritual being, totally different from magical healing, warmth, and out-of-season berries. But she wasn't about to complain.

Her feet still hurt, but the ointment soothed them, and it was much easier to walk with thick soles between her and the ground.

She returned to the creek and followed it, hoping it would lead her out of the forest. It was a cloudy day, and she couldn't tell what direction she was going. After a quarter hour, some instinct told her she was closer to Esherin than she'd been before. She was about to turn and follow the creek the other direction when something coppery brown and shimmery caught her attention.

Her eyes widened, and her sore feet darted through trees.

There, on a narrow game path, was her dress.

Kari knelt, buried her face in the fabric, and wept.

Then she followed the creek back into the forest. An hour after she passed the place where she'd been sleeping, she encountered a similar little clearing. The voice spoke to her again, this time accompanied by a rush of heat. *Stay here.*

She did.

As THE DAYS shortened and turned colder, Kari's abdomen grew larger. She'd already discarded the laces at the back of her dress. Now, the waists of her slip and her dress could only rest above her abdomen, resulting in rising hemlines and bunched-up fabric over her breasts. Well, it didn't matter if she looked funny. No one else had to look at her.

Kari spent most days gathering food. Blueberries still grew on bushes throughout the forest, always ripe. She no longer dried them, as they were frozen. And they were delicious that way, little frosty bites of sweetness. Mushrooms rounded out her diet. They shouldn't have been growing in the cold, either, but Kari just shook her head and smiled each time she came across them.

The creek was frozen, but near the tiny clearing where Kari camped was a deep pool that somehow stayed warm enough for her to bathe and do laundry.

Occasionally, Kari heard animals walking. They left her alone, even at night. But sometimes, she could swear she heard a male voice calling her name. Knowing it must be Yolin, she always found a shadowed place to hide, and she didn't think he ever got too close.

As she roamed the forest, Kari's thoughts often returned to the brothel. When memories of cruel clients flooded her mind, she instead reminisced about Mara and Dom. She hadn't expected to miss anything about Esherin House. But as she recalled Mara's wit and Dom's frequent visits to her room, she yearned to see them again. *It's just you and me*, she often told the growing baby in her womb. Sometimes, though, that didn't feel like enough.

The long winter nights were difficult to deal with. Even with the exhaustion of pregnancy, she was never tired enough to sleep the number of hours the darkness demanded. So she got in the habit of sitting in the starlight, breathing deeply, sharing whispered dreams with her child.

Sometimes it snowed, but magic shielded her from both snow and rain. She watched white flakes fall all around, close enough to reach out and touch, but they never landed on her. In heavy storms, she sat within a dome of dry warmth, surrounded by swirling white, more at peace in those moments than any other.

Days multiplied into uncounted weeks and months, and Kari's eighteenth birthday passed, though she couldn't pinpoint when. At last, tiny leaves sprouted from trees, and grass and weeds stubbornly pushed their way up through the snow. Kari brushed her finger across a pale-green leaf hanging from a low branch, then caressed her belly. "Spring is here, my child."

Her womb leapt in response, and Kari's laughter rang through the little clearing. Around the end of spring, she would give birth, right here among the trees. Here, where she was learning to love, she would teach her child the same.

Spring in the forest was sweet and pure. Birdsong filled the trees, plants burst with color, and Kari's extended belly took on a life of its own. This child, she was convinced, would be active and passionate.

Having lost track of time, Kari couldn't pinpoint when her baby should come. She knew such estimates weren't very meaningful, anyway. Her mother had always given birth early or late, never quite when she'd expected to.

What Kari had were her body's cues. And when spring had settled in long enough to proffer glimpses of summer's upcoming heat, she felt changes. Her belly was lower, taking pressure off her cramped lungs but causing her to relieve herself twice as often as usual. And the muscles in her abdomen tightened several times a day now. Hopefully it wouldn't be much longer.

One night, as Kari slept under a tree, surrounded by the warm, magical blanket that still descended on her every evening, an uncomfortable wave of tightness woke her. She lay still and tried to go back to sleep. But several minutes later, her belly was tight again, and this time, it was slightly more painful.

"Tonight, perhaps?" Kari asked the child in her womb.

The pains continued, and as the sun rose, Kari realized she had been optimistic to expect her child to come that night. Based on her level of discomfort and the irregular nature of the pains, she guessed she had hours of effort left.

She walked, stopping and leaning on trees when she needed to, frequently circling around to the creek for water. When she was hungry, she ate dried berries.

The pains continued through the day, getting more intense and closer together, but when night fell, Kari still had no reason to believe her child's arrival was imminent.

It was a cloudy night, and as much as Kari wanted to keep walking, which gave her body and mind relief, it was too dark to navigate on the uneven forest floor. She spent hours alternating between lying down, standing, and swaying against a tree as if she were dancing with it.

When the eastern sky lightened to gray, Kari released tears she'd been holding back. Her pains were sharp and strong. How much longer would this go on?

As the sun rose, clouds covered it, and soon, it began to rain. Kari was, as always, protected from the rain, but the ground was muddy, and her boots squished as she walked through the dim, unwelcoming forest.

I do not want to give birth here!

She took a few more steps.

But I have no choice.

She ate more berries, drank water from the creek, and tried to keep her spirits up.

The rain still showed no signs of abating when, in the early afternoon, Kari's pains exploded into a new level of agony. They were also longer and more frequent. She could only make it through each one by leaning her arms on a tree, pressing down like she wanted to fell the thing. She'd been silent through most of her labor, but now, she released deep, visceral moans. It was a sound different from any she'd ever heard herself make, and somehow it helped.

But as the afternoon dragged on, neither leaning nor keening made a difference anymore. Every pain felt as if it would rip her apart, and she lost whatever semblance of control she'd had, screaming through two pains and sobbing in between.

"I can't do this!" she cried to the thick, gray clouds, which were still pouring rain all around her. "I can't!"

You are doing it.

It was the same voice she'd heard when she'd seen the boots by her old rock and when she'd decided to stay in the forest. It gave her a bit of strength, enough to make it through the next pain without scream-ing. But tears still coursed down her cheeks, as incessant as the rain.

And then everything changed.

She'd wondered how she would know when it was time to give birth, but it was just as her mother had always told her. The pain itself sent Kari a message, an urgent, unmistakable one spoken to countless mothers before her: *PUSH*.

Kari was holding onto a wet, rough tree trunk, and when the new sensation hit, she dropped her hips into a squat and pushed with every bit of her strength, groaning as she did so. She filled her lungs with air, then pushed once more, long and deep, before the pain subsided.

Now, this—this, she could do. This pain was purposeful.

As Kari relished the break from the intensity of her pains, she pulled off her slip—she'd discarded her dress and underthings hours earlier—and cradled her belly with her warm arms. "You're ready, aren't you?" she whispered. "We're doing this, you and I. We're doing it together."

Another pain hit, and again, Kari fell into a squat, the backs of her thighs pressing against her leather boots. She pushed.

After several more pushing sessions, Kari leaned against the tree, the side of her belly and face pressed against it, her exhaustion making itself known. Surely this process was nearly done.

After her next pain, she realized the sun was setting. And before long, darkness descended on the third night of her labor.

"Please," she whispered to the sky.

But there was no answer, just the continuing rain.

Kari continued to push, but she couldn't tell if her work was making any difference. As the night wore on, she found she didn't have the strength to stand anymore. She lay her dress on the muddy forest floor right next to the tree. The fabric was wet, but she sat on it, rising to her hands and knees, just as she'd seen her mother do, when-ever it was time to push.

Eventually, she couldn't even make it to her hands and knees. She lay on her side, mud seeping through her dress, and cried through pain after pain, unable to add any of her own strength to her body's instinctive efforts to push her baby out.

The rain continued, water and pain and darkness coalescing, ushering her into a surreal, horrific netherworld. But at last, something changed. As Kari's body pushed, the skin between her legs burned, and something told her that her child was at long last ready to arrive.

Kari rose to a seated position, leaning against the tree trunk. And as her pain surged, she found a strength she could only attribute to magic, for it hadn't been there moments before. She pushed, and with her hands, she guided her child's head, and then its body, into the world.

Kari sobbed in relief and joy. It was dark, so dark, and she ran trembling hands over the child in her lap. First, its face.

Its face!

It had been born face-up, and Kari knew from her mother's births that most babies emerged face-down. Was that why it had taken so long?

She moved her hands along its body, then cried, "My son! My perfect, sweet son!"

Sudden realization struck Kari with the force of an ax head flying off its handle.

I am the only one crying.

She had never seen a silent newborn—well, except her mother's one stillbirth, years ago.

"No!" Kari screamed. She found the child's chest with her hand, and it was still, so still. Again, the word, a protest, a plea, left Kari's lips: "No!"

Then she pressed her lips closed, forcing her panic to flee, bringing her mind to the problem at hand. She swept a finger in the baby's mouth, just as her mother had sometimes done with her own babies, and pulled out a glob of mucus. She repeated the gesture, but the child in her hands remained still and quiet.

Swallowing her panic, Kari drew in a breath, urging her mind to find solutions.

He's not breathing. But I am.

She didn't know if it would work, but she picked him up, body in one hand, head in the other, and brought her mouth to his.

He was so tiny that her mouth covered both his mouth and his nose. Kari sobbed a breath into her baby's mouth, then pulled her head back, forcing herself to stop crying as she drew in more air. She again covered the child's mouth and nose with her own and breathed into him, with more control this time. Another inhale, and another shared breath. Another. And another.

The wail of a newborn cut through the rain, bouncing off tree bark, smashing into Kari's heart, breaking it into ragged, exquisite pieces.

She joined her own cries to his as she pulled him to her chest, both their voices rising to the dark clouds. Joy and indignation melded together in the same harmonious song created by mothers and newborns across every generation.

He stopped crying first, and a moment later, Kari's sobs halted with a gasp. An odd glow was emanating from her son's body, unlike anything she'd seen before.

She pulled him away from her, cradling him over her lap. Golden light filled the center of his little chest, the glow illuminating the sheets of rain falling around them.

Kari's breaths came faster as she watched the light move down her child's arms, all the way to his hands. They glowed brightly, rays of gold shimmering from every tiny crevice of his wrinkled fingers and palms, the sight both lovely and strange.

Kari's breathing slowed as she basked in the beauty of her son and the indescribable magic inhabiting him. Then the odd light traveled back the way it had come. The child's hands, then arms, faded, again blending with the surrounding blackness. The glow only inhabited his chest, as it had at the beginning. Finally, it dimmed to nothing, leaving mother and son in the dark again.

Kari couldn't fathom what the light was. All she knew was her son had been brought back from the brink of death, and then that strange glow had entered his body.

Surely Sava's hand was on this child.

"Savala," she whispered to the baby, who was quiet now. It was a common name, meaning "Son of Sava," but it fit this child in a way it had never fit any of the bratty little Savalas Kari had grown up with, not to mention the Savala who'd often visited her at the brothel. No, this child was truly Sava's son, touched by him, alive for a purpose. "Savala," she breathed again.

She brought him to her breast and winced as he latched on. Then, as her son ate his first meal, Kari became aware of the raindrops falling on both of them and the cool air chilling her body. Her shield against rain was gone, along with her magical blanket.

She couldn't guess why the magic had fled, but she held her child closer, determined that he wouldn't get cold if she could help it. The rain continued as Kari's body expelled the afterbirth.

She was bleeding, and she had no way to cut her son's cord, but she'd deal with all that when the sun came up. For now, she needed to warm her baby. She found the slip she'd discarded earlier. It was wet and muddy, but it was better than nothing. She wrapped it around Savala.

He drifted off while eating, his chest rising and falling in perfect rhythm against Kari's breast. She lay on her muddy, wet dress, holding her son close to her. Despite the rain and her afterpains, exhaustion took over, and she joined Savala in sleep.

A SOUND JARRED Kari out of her deep slumber. Eyes still closed, she murmured, "Sweet baby, you hungry?"

She reached out for Savala, but her hand landed instead on her wet dress.

Her eyes flung themselves open. Yolin was at the edge of the clearing, dashing into the trees. And Savala was gone.

Kari leapt to her feet, not caring that she was wearing nothing but boots. She had to get her son.

She ran into the trees, screaming, "Yolin, stop! I'll do whatever you want! Stop!"

He laughed and kept going.

The purposeful rage of a protective mother swelled within Kari, but two days and three nights of labor had stolen her strength. Her breaths didn't want to fill her lungs. Her legs were ribbons, ready to collapse to the ground. She forced herself to keep going.

"Yolin!" she cried.

He didn't respond, just ran ahead, getting farther away with each determined step.

Darkness threatened the edges of Kari's vision. "Sava, help me!"

But this time, the mysterious god and his magic were far away. Blackness continued to intrude, and then Kari's legs stopped working. She fell to her knees, bringing her hands to the ground. Her entire body was trembling. She pushed herself up, but her legs refused the effort, falling back to the forest floor.

"Savala!" Kari moaned, just before she passed out.

When she woke, she didn't know if it had been seconds or minutes. But Yolin was out of sight. He had her child, and she had no hope of catching up.

"Why?" she begged the sky, which was now cloudless and bright blue.

The sun mocked her with searing silence.

CHAPTER FIVE

The children dropped their sticks and ran, but hope fled their hearts. Even were they strong and healthy, children could never outrun a bear.

And what a bear this was, a giantess even when she returned her front paws to the ground. Strong sinews drove her across the dirt toward the children as her cry proclaimed her vigor and strength.

-from The Origin of Wild Magic *by Edoren the Bard*

KARI SLEPT where she'd fallen. Rest was the last thing she wanted, but it wasn't optional.

She woke in the afternoon, utterly empty—of hope, of sustenance, of her child. Questions drifted lazily through her mind: *How did Yolin find me after all this time?* During her long months in the forest, she'd suspected magic was shielding her from him. *Why didn't magic protect my child?*

Standing, she gazed down at her body. Her belly was still swollen. She was bleeding, and that wouldn't stop for weeks. She itched from dozens of insect bites. Until today, she hadn't gotten one bite in all the months she'd been here. It was more proof that her magical protection had fled.

Why now? Kari didn't have an answer, but one thing was clear. *Sava finally realized I'm not worth the trouble.*

She shook her arms, as if releasing her dependence on magic. She had to get her son back. If there were any chance of it working, she'd run into the city right now. But she was wearing only socks and boots; she'd be driven out of town or arrested. She had to take care of a few things before she could journey back to the city.

Kari walked to her campsite, the swollen skin between her legs aching with every step. Her slip was gone, wrapped around her son, but her dress waited under the tree where she'd given birth. Mud and blood caked the fabric. She lifted it and walked to her little pool.

Stepping into the water, she gasped. It had always been magically warm; now, it sent shivers through her whole body. Teeth gritted, she waded in until it reached her waist.

The dress wouldn't come clean; she was sure of that. But she placed it on a stone and used a smaller rock to scrub out as much of the mud and blood as she could. Then she rinsed it and repeated the process over and over until she convinced herself she couldn't get the fabric any cleaner without scrubbing holes in it.

By then, Kari was used to the water. It felt soothing to her skin where she was sore from the birth. It had washed her legs clean of blood. But her heart still felt filthy, encrusted with self-wrought defeat.

I failed as a daughter and a sister. I sold my body to whoever would pay, and a stranger impregnated me. And now I've committed the ultimate sin, failing to protect my helpless child.

Kari cried as she fell to her knees. She lowered her whole head into the water, wishing she could inhale the cool liquid and let it cleanse her on the inside, ending her suffering.

She lifted her head and breathed the warm air instead. Possibly she was a terrible mother. But she couldn't leave Savala in Roza's and Yolin's hands. She didn't want to imagine what they'd do to the son of a runaway prostitute.

So she stepped out of the pool, ignoring the pain left over from her long labor and difficult birth, carrying her wet dress with her. She lay it on the stone she had used for months to dry clothing and berries. It wasn't as flat or large as the stone she'd had at her original camp, but it did the trick.

The dress was designed for beauty, not practicality. It had a sheer shawl of sorts attached at the shoulders, draping down the wearer's arms and back. Kari had a better use for it now. She tore it off the dress and threaded it through her legs and around her middle, below her swollen abdomen. It was a poor replacement for the absorbent rags she was used to, and it wouldn't stanch her bleeding for long. She'd have to find another option soon. She put on her pantalettes, which she'd had the forethought to drape over a tree branch early in labor. The long, cotton pants were wet, but not muddy. They were tight these days, and they held the sheer fabric in place.

She combed her hair, a task that felt indulgent at such a time. But her goal was to be as inconspicuous as possible in case anyone saw her, and after three nights and two days of labor, her hair was a mess.

That done, Kari ate the rest of the berries she'd saved. She was still famished afterward, and somehow she knew she wouldn't find any blueberry bushes today.

She put on her wet dress. Shoulders squared, she stepped into the trees and pointed her steps toward the city.

THE SECOND KARI saw people on the streets, she dashed back to the forest. There simply wasn't any good way to sneak up on the brothel during the day. So she waited near the edge of the trees, impatiently watching the sky.

Once it was dark, she wandered along the back of a residential street until she found a clothesline with clean laundry waving in the light breeze. Looking around to be sure no one was watching, she snagged several socks, along with a man's shirt, before darting back to the trees. She discarded the dirty fabric between her legs and remade her diaper with the shirt, this time putting socks inside it to add extra absorption. It was uncomfortable and bulky, but it would work. She shoved the extra socks in her bodice, knowing it looked ridiculous and hoping it was too dark for anyone to notice.

Kari took a deep breath and returned to the big house she'd hoped to never see again. She approached from the rear. Esherin House was at the end of the street and sat on a larger lot than the other businesses. Instead of backing right up to the sewer trench, it had a nice-sized back yard.

Kari passed the kitchen where she'd taken countless baths, relieved not to see anyone through its windows. Stepping up to the house, she looked up at the women's bedrooms on the second floor. Candlelight shone from the windows, and she swallowed down tears for the women working in those little rooms.

There were other rooms across the hall. Kari had lived in one of them and had hated its dark, dreary atmosphere. But Mara brought in enough income to be awarded a window room. Her shutters were open to let in the evening air, and shadows moved along the top part of the far wall. A few minutes later, one shadow stood. Kari could just make out a man's head as he opened the door and exited the room.

She threw a small rock toward the open window but missed, hitting the stone above it. She tried again, then again. The fourth time, she was successful, but there was no response. She kept throwing little rocks into the room until at last, a figure appeared in the window.

Mara's voice was loud. "Who's down there?"

"It's me." Kari kept her voice quiet.

"Who?"

"Shh! It's me. Come down, please."

Mara left the window for a few seconds, returning with a candle. She held it out the window, then leaned over the sill.

Kari's heart thudded as she stepped up to the building, allowing the candlelight to fall on her face.

"Kari!" Mara whispered.

"Come down," Kari begged.

Another voice emanated from Mara's room, this one masculine. "Hey, beautiful, haven't seen you in a while!"

Mara left the window, and Kari huddled against the side of the building, trying to block out noises from above that brought back memories she thought she'd buried.

Perhaps a quarter hour later, Mara's voice emerged from the room again. "Are you still there?"

Kari stood. "Yes."

"You know I can't come down until my evening work is done. And how do you expect me to leave the house? Between Yolin, Roza, and the maid, someone always hears if a door opens."

Kari hadn't thought that far ahead. The ceilings downstairs were high, the upstairs windows unsafe to jump from—all by design, she was convinced.

"I'll work on a way to get you out the window," Kari whispered.

"Fine. I'll come back when we shut down for the night."

Mara left the window, and Kari stole behind the neighboring buildings. The passage there looked just like the one across the street where Kari had run from Yolin months earlier. A narrow strip of land separated the inns and pubs from the buildings on the street behind them, and a sewer trench took up much of the space.

This time, however, Kari wasn't running. She crept along the edge of the trench, using what little illumination the stars provided and testing every step before she put her foot down.

At the third building down, a pub, she found what she was looking for. Wooden crates were stacked between the pub's rear wall and the trench. Kari picked up one of them and carried it back to the space behind the brothel. She set it upside down under Mara's window and went back for another.

The task was slow; Kari would not risk injuring her ankle in the putrid sewer trench again. As she carried one crate after another—first from the pub and then from an inn farther down the street—she thought about Mara, wondering how many men she had to entertain that night. *I'd rather be bleeding and sore, carrying these crates along the edge of a sewer, than doing Mara's work.*

At last, she'd assembled a set of tall stairs made of crates. Mara would still have to lower herself a few feet to reach the first crate, but Kari thought it would work.

In the deep stillness of night, when the brothel was at last closed for the evening, Mara reappeared. She stared for several seconds at the crates. "This doesn't look safe."

Kari had kept control of her emotions since leaving the forest, but now a sob thrust its way between her lips into the quiet darkness. She wasn't sure what had triggered it—the sight of her friend or the threat of all her work being for naught—but she saw Mara's shoulders drop at the sound.

"Oh, fine, I'll try," Mara said. She left her candle burning in the room, and its light illuminated her as she turned and swung one leg over the windowsill. "I can't reach!"

"You're almost there!"

Mara stretched her leg down, and her toe hit the crate. She lowered herself farther, standing on it first with one felt-and-velvet slipper, then the other. Still gripping the windowsill, she cautiously turned her whole body to face Kari.

"You're doing it," Kari said.

Mara huffed, released the windowsill, and lowered herself to a squat, then sat on the top crate. She pushed herself to the next step, then the next. It was still several feet off the ground, but she slid off, bending her knees as she landed.

"Well done!" Kari said.

Mara enveloped her old friend in a tight hug. "What are you doing back here?"

"Come with me," Kari whispered. "We need to talk."

Mara pulled back, then reached out and touched a sock sticking out of Kari's dress. "What in the world is this?"

THEY SETTLED on the dirt next to a pub that had been closed for months.

"I had my baby," Kari said.

"When?" Mara asked. "Where is it?"

Kari gritted her teeth, waiting to answer until she'd shoved her emotion back into her gut, where it burned like a hot iron. When she knew she could answer without crying, she said, "He was born last night. Yolin found me in the forest and took him away from me."

"Oh, Kari."

Mara reached out, but Kari put her hands up, preventing the hug.

"I can't cry right now. I—I don't know how Yolin found me right when my son was born. But I have to get him back."

Grabbing her hand, Mara said, "Yolin's been looking for you in the forest for months. Sometimes he'd see you from far away, but he could never catch you. He'd come home, ranting and raving, saying it seemed like something was keeping you away from him."

Kari swallowed. "Magic. It protected me."

Both women were silent. A toad croaked nearby.

"I wondered if it was something like that," Mara finally whispered. "But I didn't think that sort of thing happened to people like us."

"Neither did I." Kari's voice was hard. "But when my son was born, the magic stopped." She didn't say anything about the strange glow Savala had experienced, fearing Mara would think she was crazy. She couldn't help but wonder, though, if there was a connection between the magic that had filled her son and her loss of protection. Whatever the explanation, she couldn't think of anything crueler than Sava withdrawing magic when she needed it the most.

"After you left, Roza found the paper where you tracked your cycles," Mara said. "So when she knew you were due to give birth soon, she started sending Yolin out to look for you every morning. Sometimes he didn't come back until dark. They're obsessed with you, Kari. They couldn't stand to know that you'd escaped. All they could talk about was finding you and taking your baby."

Kari pushed words through her tight, protesting throat. "Well, they succeeded."

"Oh, Kari."

Again, Mara tried to hug her, and again, Kari resisted. "Do you have any idea where my son is?"

Mara didn't answer, and when Kari grabbed her friend's hand, she found it tightened into a fist.

"What do you know, Mara?" Kari asked.

"We all want our babies." Since the day Mara's own child had been stolen, her voice had often taken on this hollow tone, all hope drained from it. "You can't get him back, Kari."

"You know something!" It took all Kari's strength not to scream and shake Mara by the shoulders until the truth tumbled out. "Tell me!"

Mara shifted, turning toward Kari. It was too dark to see her expression, but her voice was full of tight intensity.

"One of the women of the house heard Roza and Yolin talking about how much Mayor Held and his wife would pay for a baby. But he's the most powerful man in the city, and you'll never win if you take him on. He might kill you. Do you hear me, Kari? Your son is gone. You can't get him back."

Kari's breaths quickened. "Where does the mayor live?"

Mara gripped Kari's shoulders, her fingers digging in painfully. "Didn't you hear me? You can't go!"

"If you don't tell me, I'll ask around town, and that's bound to get back to Roza and Yolin." Kari's voice was low and steady.

Silence descended again, and at last, Mara sighed, her fingers loosening. "It's the big stone house on the hill at the north side of the city. You can't miss it."

Kari stood. "Thank you, Mara."

"Wait!" Mara scrambled to her feet.

Kari was already walking off, but she stopped and turned. "I'm not changing my mind."

"I know. I have some rags you can use. For the bleeding. And I can give you one of my old dresses, too."

One tear escaped Kari's eye, and she brushed it away, swallowing hard. "Thanks."

They walked back toward the brothel. When it came in sight, Mara added, "Oh, and I'm sorry, Kari, but you'll have to move those crates once I'm back in my room. Nobody can see them in the morning."

Kari released a sigh and nodded.

THREE-QUARTERS OF AN HOUR LATER, Kari was in fresh clothes, and she'd stashed the crates in the same place she and Mara had sat and talked. They'd be easily accessible there if Kari needed to rebuild the makeshift staircase.

She was sore and utterly exhausted. But her baby might be nearby, and she wasn't about to wait any longer to find him. She walked through the dark streets toward the north side of the city.

When she reached her destination, Kari clenched her teeth and swallowed back tears. The hill rose high above the rest of the city, and she didn't dare walk on the dirt road that snaked up it. Most of the slope was wooded, and Kari stepped back into trees that reminded her of the forest she'd just left. She kept the road in sight as she walked.

Her plan was to hike nonstop until she reached the big house at the top, but her tired limbs and sore body didn't allow it. She stopped frequently, wishing for water or food.

At one point, Kari released a small squeal when the starlight illuminated a twillberry bush on her path. She plucked two of the lumpy berries and, ignoring how hard they were, popped them in her mouth. Her face and jaw muscles tightened at the tart, bitter flavor. If it had been daytime, she would've known these berries weren't even close to ripe. But she continued to pick them, scowling with every bite, determined to eat a little food.

By the time Kari reached the top of the hill, dawn was peeking its golden head over the horizon in the east. She'd hoped to complete her trek when it was still dark. But the house was in sight. She couldn't stop now.

Kari crept through the woods, circling wide around the house until she faced its rear. It was huge, even bigger than the brothel, and its stone exterior gave it the look of a fortress.

No time like the present.

Kari left the trees, suppressing her hesitation with every quiet step. She crossed the open lawn behind the home, passing a stable and other outbuildings along the way. No one stopped her as she approached the home itself.

The shutters were closed, but the sweetest sound Kari could imagine suddenly emanated from the big building. Even a few hours with Savala had been enough for her to know his cry.

Kari fell to her knees, trying to control her own sobs. When her crying slowed, she heard the muffled voices of a man and woman, also upstairs. If she was going to sneak in and get her baby, she couldn't do it now. She had to wait until everyone was sleeping. Kari clenched her fists, wishing she had something to punch, and began walking through the gentle dawn light, back toward the trees.

"Gettin' low on water, aren't you?"

The gruff, male voice had come from the stable. A tingling jolt of fear burst from Kari's chest into her hands and feet. She ran over open ground toward the trees.

"Hey!" the same voice shouted.

Oh no, Sava, no!

"Hey!" he called again.

Then Kari saw him in her peripheral vision, running toward her. She tried to put on another burst of speed, but she hadn't thought to lift her skirts, and even as she grasped at them, they slowed her down, threatening to trip her.

A third "Hey!" reached her ears half a second before a hand grabbed her arm. Kari tried to keep running, but her captor was too strong, and her boots skidded to a stop in the dewy grass.

She faced the man holding her. He was tall and strong, not quite middle-aged. A trimmed beard, brighter red than her hair, surrounded his mouth. His eyes narrowed as he examined her.

"Who are you? What are you doing here?"

Kari swallowed, a difficult task due to her dry mouth. Her voice was hoarse when she responded with the only thing that came to mind: "Are you Mayor Held?"

The man's face softened a little, amusement sneaking out of his wary eyes. "I'm his groom. Well, his horses' groom. Why are you here?"

She opened her mouth, but all that came out was a croak.

"You sound sick."

She shook her head. "Just thirsty."

His eyebrows rose, and he studied her for several seconds. At last, he said, "Not sure why you're up on this hill, but you need something to drink. If I bring you in the stable, will you stay there while I get water from the well? I have to water the horses, anyway."

Kari nodded.

"I'll be able to see you from the well, so if you run, I'll catch you again. You understand I can't just let you go when you're trespassing on the mayor's property, right?"

Another nod. "Will you let go of my arm?"

The man gave her a good stare before nodding gruffly and letting her go. He led her to the stable and beckoned her in.

Several candles in the building provided enough light for Kari to see six occupied horse stalls, a storage room, and a ladder leading up to a second floor. She approached the first horse, who watched her with impassive eyes as he chewed. Kari looked down and saw the trough of oats behind the wooden stall door.

Food.

She slid her hand down the inside of the door but couldn't quite reach the oats. Standing on her tiptoes, she tried harder, groaning as the wood dug into the soft skin under her arm, irritating an insect bite.

"What you doing now, Miss?"

Kari started, pulled her arm back to her side, and spun to look at the man. She kept her mouth shut.

"Trying to get some oats? You hungry?"

Kari nodded.

The man set his full water bucket next to Kari. "Don't drink from the bucket now; I'm getting you a cup." He walked to the storage room, keeping his eyes on her for all but the few seconds he was in the room, and returned with a carved wooden cup.

Kari dipped it in the water and drank it down—once, twice, a third time. "Thank you."

"Let me finish watering the horses, and then I'll take you upstairs. I've got real food up there. You don't want those oats. They're probably full of horse spittle." He gave her a gentle smile before emptying the bucket into one of the horse troughs and taking it back outside.

It took several minutes for him to water all the horses, but when he finished, he was true to his word. Grabbing a candle, he beckoned Kari to the ladder.

What's he going to do to me up there? As soon as the thought came to her mind, she shoved it away. Probably nothing other men hadn't done to her. Maybe if she told him she'd just given birth, he wouldn't want anything. And if he did, at least she'd get food in return this time. She followed him up the ladder.

He gestured for her to sit at the table, and when she did, he joined her. Half a loaf of bread sat upright with its cut edge on the table, accompanied by a cheese wheel and a knife.

I could grab the knife, kill him, eat his food, and escape.

But before Kari could get her courage up, he'd picked up the knife.

With unhurried hands, he pulled the food toward him. "Name's Rusk," he said, cutting through the bread's thick crust. "Been working here for nearly a decade now. Not a bad place, all in all. Sure is a rough trek up and down the hill, though." He looked up, met her gaze, and looked back down. When he was done cutting the bread, he handed the slice to her. "Sorry I don't have any butter."

"Thank you." She set to work on it, not minding the lack of butter. It was a little stale, but it was delicious.

"My pleasure." He took the knife to the cheese and continued, "I'm impressed you climbed up here on foot. Or I assume you did. I didn't see any horses around, and I don't think you're hiding wings under that dress." He smiled at her again, then returned his attention to the cheese, trimming off the hard edges. "Here you go."

She took the thick slice of cheese and ate a bite. "Aren't you going to eat, too?"

"Already did, before the sun came up."

"Oh." She finished her food in silence.

Without asking if she wanted seconds, he cut more bread and cheese and set it before her.

She ate it quickly, and when she'd finished, she cleared her throat. "I suppose you want something in return. But you should know—"

Rusk interrupted, "What exactly would I want in return, Miss?"

Kari looked down at the low neck of the dress she'd borrowed from Mara. "I'm sure you noticed this isn't the type of dress a nice woman wears. But—"

The man held up a hand, and Kari stopped talking.

"I haven't known you long enough to judge if you're nice or

mean," he said, "but I do know this: I'm a nice man. You can keep that pretty dress on."

Tears darted into Kari's eyes, one of them slipping out before she could stop it. She wiped it away. "I guess I should go, then," she murmured. "Thank you for the food and for . . . for your kindness." She stood.

"When's the baby due?"

Kari froze.

"Oh, my, I'm sorry. My mother always told me not to ask that question unless I was sure. I'm sorry if you're not expecting."

Her legs again unsteady, Kari dropped back into her chair and rested her hand on her swollen midsection. "He was born two nights ago." She didn't know why she told him that. Maybe she felt sorry for his embarrassment.

Rusk's mouth opened into a perfect circle. "You climbed up that hill and you just had a baby?"

She nodded.

"Where's the child?"

Kari didn't answer, but without meaning to, she shifted her eyes in the direction of the house. She dragged her gaze back to Rusk.

He blinked, and his eyes were shining. "Is that your baby in the big house?"

"Yes." An unexpected sob accompanied her response.

"Did you—did you ask them to care for your baby?"

"No." Kari forced the words through her shuddering throat. "They took him."

" Well . . . oh my, that's not right, is it? For them to have your child? Not right at all."

Kari pressed her palm hard against her mouth, trying to keep the sobs from escaping.

Rusk sat up straight, then moved his index finger up to his mouth. "Shh." The sound barely brushed the air between them.

Kari heard what must have had caught Rusk's attention—footsteps below. The shock of it squelched her tears.

"Rusk, I told you I was leaving just after dawn!" a man called. "Saddle my horse!"

"So sorry, Mayor! Be right there!" Rusk stood and walked to Kari, bringing his mouth down to nearly touch her ear. "Please stay. I'll be back, and I'll help you. There's a bag of rags in that corner there if you need any." He pointed. "Put dirty ones in the empty bag." Not waiting for a response, he lowered himself down the ladder.

Kari listened to the men talking. How had Rusk known she'd need rags? As she'd climbed the hill, she'd used up all the ones Mara had given her. Keeping her movements quiet, she replaced dirty rags with clean ones, then sat at the table, waiting.

She knew she shouldn't believe a stranger would help her. But something told her Rusk would follow through. *If he comes up that ladder alone, I'll trust him.*

Perhaps a quarter hour later, he did come up, and he was alone. Wordlessly, he again sat across from her.

Kari held out a hand and met his eyes. "My name is Kari."

CHAPTER SIX

*The bear's hot breath fell on the children as she roared once more, reaching out
a paw larger than their heads, intent on the kill.*

*Expecting death at any moment, Alena and Alaya did not cease their
sprinting until a new sound reached their ears, the agonized scream of the
creature behind them.*

-from The Origin of Wild Magic *by Edoren the Bard*

Rusk took her hand in both of his and squeezed gently before letting it
go. "Kari, I once had a wife. A baby, too." He blinked several times,
looking to the side, before turning his gaze back on her. "Remember
the fever that came through here fourteen years ago? Well . . ." He
pressed his lips together, and his freckled throat rippled as he swallowed hard. "I'm glad I can help a young mother and child," he
concluded, his voice strained.

"Thank you," Kari whispered.

Rusk took a deep breath and gave her a shaky smile. "You must be tired as a bear in winter. My bed is comfortable enough. There's a chamber pot in there, too. You sleep while I care for the horses and do other things around the property. If you wake up, get yourself more bread and cheese. I'll refill your water cup." He paused, locking eyes with Kari. "And tonight—we'll get your baby back."

When that sank in, Kari wanted to rush to Rusk and hug him. But he was already on the ladder. Minutes later, she was settled in his bed under warm blankets, and she slept as soon as her eyes closed.

When she woke, light filtered past the shutters of the little window. It was just as dim as it had been when she'd gone to bed. Had she really only rested a few minutes?

She stepped out of bed and opened the shutters. The light was coming from the west now, not the east. She'd slept the day away.

Rusk was nowhere to be seen. Kari replaced soaked rags with clean ones and sat down at the table. It felt rude eating this man's food, but she was too hungry to be polite. She cut herself two more slices of bread and an extra-thick wedge of cheese, then washed down her feast with the water Rusk had left for her.

When she was done, she returned to bed, feeling a little guilty for being so lazy but knowing she'd need energy to get her baby and transport him safely down the big hill. She closed her eyes and savored the quiet serenity.

Eventually, quiet footsteps caught Kari's attention. She slipped out of bed and crept to the doorway of the little bedroom. Rusk was lighting two candles at the table. He looked up. "You get some rest?"

"Yes. Thank you."

"The cook gave me some ham. Would you like some?"

Ham. Kari hadn't had one bite of meat since leaving the brothel the first time. With magic sustaining her, she'd barely missed it, but since Savala's birth, she'd been craving meat. Unable to squelch her smile, she nearly ran to the table.

Rusk chuckled. "I guess that's a yes."

She watched his gentle hands as he sliced the ham, and she was glad she hadn't found the courage to attack him with that knife. Since first arriving in Esherin, the only good man she'd met was Dom. There was a certain comfort in realizing he wasn't the only one.

They ate and talked about how Kari might get her son back. When the meal and planning were done, they sat in near silence, only breaking it with occasional, short chats. Kari had grown used to the quiet during her months in the forest, and she appreciated Rusk for not prying into her past.

They sat for hours past dark, and finally, Rusk said, "I'm sure everyone's in bed now. Let's go to the house."

How could he be so calm? Kari's heart threatened to either leap out of her chest or stop beating altogether. She pushed herself up from her chair and gave Rusk a smile she hoped was brave. "Let's go."

It was a cooler night than the previous one, and Kari shivered when she stepped outside.

"You're cold," Rusk said. "Come on back in."

She did, and he scampered up the ladder, returning seconds later with a cloak. He held it out to her.

"I can't take your cloak!"

"I can get another. You'll need to keep your baby warm, too."

She couldn't argue with that. The thick, canvas cloak was rough and stiff, but she knew she'd appreciate it when fall arrived. Raising a child in the woods would be challenging without magic. At that thought, a flicker of doubt lit up her mind, but she rid herself of it with a shake of the head. Savala needed his mother. She'd find a way to care for him.

They walked silently to the back of the house. Kari lowered herself into a squat next to the back stoop.

Rusk walked to a window several feet away. He tapped on the shutters. When there was no answer, he knocked a little harder.

"Who's there?" a wary female voice called.

"It's me. Rusk."

A shutter swung open. Kari couldn't see who was in the window, but Rusk had told her the room belonged to the cook. The woman said, "Do you have any idea how late it is, Rusk?"

"I know. I'm really sorry. Think I mighta left my cloak inside the house when I was getting food earlier."

"What use you got for a cloak at night?"

"I sleep in it."

"Men." Kari could almost hear the woman's head shake. "I'll open the back door for you; give me a minute."

"Thanks."

Soon the door rattled, then opened.

"I really appreciate this," Kari heard Rusk say. "If you give me the key, I'll lock up. That way you can go back to bed. I'll give you the key tomorrow."

"Are you sure? I'll get in trouble if this door is open come morning."

"I promise."

"You silly man, did you come without a candle?"

"I've always been able to see well in the dark."

"Whatever you say. Come on in."

Kari watched as the door swung shut. She shivered, from fear rather than cold, and sent a quiet prayer up to the starry sky.

The door opened again, and Rusk's head and hand appeared. He beckoned Kari, and she stood and followed him in, trying to keep her boots silent.

Rusk's breath was warm on Kari's ear as he whispered, "Walk down that hall to the left. Take the servant's stairs to the second floor."

He turned to leave, and Kari stopped him with a hand on his arm. He brought his ear down to her mouth, and she whispered, "I can't thank you enough."

"You need anything, you know where to find me."

He left, pulling the door silently closed, and Kari didn't hesitate. She walked down the hall, holding her breath as she passed closed doors, probably more servants' bedrooms. When she reached the staircase at the end of the hall, she breathed again.

The stairs were intolerably squeaky, but she made it to the top undetected. Kari opened the door at the top of the stairs and emerged into another hallway.

Based on what she'd heard when she'd first arrived, she thought Savala was in the back corner room at the same side of the house where she now stood. Rusk had said Mrs. Held's room was right next to that. Kari took a cautious step toward the room, then another.

Her pace was painfully slow, but it allowed her to adjust her steps any time a floorboard started to squeak. She made it to the door of the first room, took a slow, deep breath to compensate for her racing heart, and put her hand on the latch.

Press down. Careful—Careful—That's it. There was a slight click, and the door swung open.

A small crib was barely visible across the large, dark bedroom, below the window. Tears pressed against Kari's eyes and throat, but she forbade them from exiting. Every instinct in her screamed that she should dash in and snatch up her son, running with him until they reached the trees. But caution won out, and she stepped even more carefully than she had in the hallway.

She was halfway across the room when she heard a groan and the sound of a body shifting in bed—not from the crib, but farther to the right. Kari froze.

"That you, ma'am?" a sleepy, female voice asked.

Whoever this was, she probably thought Kari was the mayor's wife. "Mmm hmm," Kari said in a voice so soft, she hoped the other woman couldn't tell who it was.

"If the baby's hungry, let me know."

The wet nurse! Until that moment, Kari hadn't even thought about who was feeding her son. Gratitude and jealousy warred in her heart toward the woman performing the crucial duty that should belong to her. Again, Kari heard the woman shift in bed, and then everything was silent.

She continued her journey across the room, walking at a normal speed. She had to get Savala out before the sleepy nurse took a closer look at her.

Then she was at the crib, and there he was, the gentle glow of starlight illuminating him. Overpowering, liquid joy burst out of Kari's eyes. Swallowing each sob before it could escape, she reached out and picked up her son, bringing him to her chest.

Savala was warm and soft and tinier than she'd remembered. The rise and fall of his chest against hers brought her back to the moment when she'd breathed life into him, and the next moment when that strange glow had overtaken his chest and hands.

As much as Kari would have liked to stand there for hours, holding her son, forgetting about the rest of the world, practical concerns shoved past her bliss. They had to leave.

She turned and walked toward the door, one silent step at a time. It was still partially open, but with the baby in her arms, she needed a wider space. She pulled the door toward her, wincing when the hinges creaked.

But the squeak of aged hinges was nothing compared to the wail that suddenly burst from Savala, piercing the room's black silence.

Kari swung the door all the way open and ran through it, ignoring the questions of the nurse behind her. She darted to the head of the stairs, but before she could pass through the open doorway, a second woman's voice said, "What's going on?"

Once again, Kari ran encumbered by thick skirts. She hurried down the long staircase, wishing she could take the steps three or four at a time, but unwilling to take such a chance with the priceless cargo she carried. One hand on the banister, one on her screaming baby, she clomped down the squeaky steps, sure the whole house was now awake.

A man's voice sounded from the floor above, and then, when Kari had nearly reached the bottom of the long staircase, she heard someone following—someone who, from the sound of it, had no qualms about leaping down several steps at a time.

She ran into the hallway, legs tangling in her skirt. Savala's heartbreaking cry wasn't loud enough to muffle the footsteps that now joined her on the ground floor. But she was almost there; she could see the hallway that led to the back door, just ahead—

A few feet in front of Kari, a door opened, and a woman in a nightcap and robe stepped out. "What—" the servant began.

Kari didn't slow. She thought she could barrel past the servant, shove her to the side. But the servant's eyes widened, and she held her arms out like a human fence. It was just enough to make Kari hesitate. And just enough for her pursuer to catch up.

Kari's head snapped back, and she nearly fell. Someone had her hair. She tried to pull away, but it was no use. The servant was still blocking the way, and the grip on her hair was firm.

"Stop!" The voice behind Kari was male. "Stop fighting, I say! You'll drop the baby!"

Kari almost laughed. She'd die before dropping her son. She spun her body around, which brought her face-to-chest with the tall man holding her hair in one hand and a candle in the other.

Oh, dear Sava, no. She knew this man. He'd visited her at the brothel several times. She knew those pale eyes and scratchy, blonde beard. He was rough, never hurting her in any way that could get him in trouble with Roza, but always treating her as a possession he didn't much like. Was this Mayor Held?

Kari took a deep breath and shouted, "This is my baby!" Her spittle hit his nightshirt.

His entire face was hard, the corners of his mouth downturned and the skin between his eyes compressed into sharp pleats. "Not anymore." He still had her hair, and he twisted and pulled, yanking Kari's head back and bringing his face close to hers. "You're coming back upstairs with me. Will you walk, or should I drag you?"

Kari imagined her body bouncing up the hard steps, Savala crying with every jolt. She closed her eyes tightly, then forced them back open. "I'll walk."

"Good choice." The man looked past Kari and spoke to the servant, raising his voice above Savala's cries. "Send my delivery boy upstairs in five minutes."

"Yes, sir."

The man didn't let go of Kari's hair, but he stopped pulling on it, using it as a loose leash as he directed her down the hall, up the stairs, and past the nursery. The door next to it was open, and a woman stood there in her nightgown, backlit by candlelight.

"Everything's fine," the man said. "The wet nurse was getting tired, so we've brought in someone to help. You can go back to bed." He continued walking, not waiting for a response.

That confirmed it. The man propelling Kari forward was Mayor Held, and the woman was his wife. Kari's breaths came faster, and she held Savala even tighter. He was still crying.

Mayor Held shoved Kari into his room. He let go of her hair and pointed at an upholstered chair in the corner farthest from the door. "Sit."

She obeyed, and the door slammed.

"Feed the baby," Mayor Held ordered.

She looked down. The dress certainly wasn't made for nursing.

"What are you waiting for?" Still holding his candle, Mayor Held walked up to her. He must have seen the answer in her expression, because his mouth twisted into a cruel smile. "Embarrassed, are you? I've seen a lot more of you than that."

Then he watched as Kari leaned forward, hoping the big cloak would cast enough shadow to provide some privacy. She unbuttoned the front of her dress and began nursing Savala. His crying stopped.

Mayor Held knelt in front of Kari. He reached out a soft hand and squeezed her cheeks together hard. Her teeth dug into the sensitive flesh inside her mouth. It was degrading and cruel, and it took all Kari's presence of mind not to slap him.

"If my wife is stupid enough to come in here, you won't mention to her that we've met before. Not if you want to survive the night. Understand?"

Kari nodded.

"I want to hear you say it."

He was still pinching her cheeks, and she murmured, "Yes" through her pursed lips.

Mayor Held laughed. "Good girl."

He stood and walked around the room, using his candle to light several others in wall sconces. Then he sat at his desk and began to write. Just as he finished, there was a knock at the door.

"Enter!" the mayor called.

A bleary-eyed young man came in. His eyes fell on her, and he didn't look away.

"Just a woman feeding my baby, nothing to stare at," Mayor Held snapped.

The young man shifted his gaze back to the mayor.

"Take a horse, and deliver this note," the mayor said.

"When?"

"Now."

"Sir," the delivery boy said, "it's dark."

"I'm not blind." The mayor walked to the boy, stood over him, and held out the note. "Go."

"Yes, sir."

The boy left, closing the door behind him.

"I'm going to get some work done, and you're going to keep your mouth shut and take care of my baby while we wait." Mayor Held's voice was casual and almost friendly. He sat at his desk.

"Wait for what?" Kari asked.

He looked up and met her gaze, that terrible smile filling his face again. "You'll see."

THE CLOCK on Mayor Held's mantle chimed every hour. It had just struck for the third time when a knock at last sounded at the bedroom door. Kari started; she was slumped in the chair, still holding Savala tightly, and had been trying unsuccessfully not to doze.

"Enter," the mayor called.

The person who entered held a candle to the side, and it wasn't until she took several steps that the light in the room illuminated her enough for Kari to recognize her.

Roza.

Roza, however, wasn't looking at Kari. She focused only on Mayor Held. "Why in the world did you need to fetch me in the middle of the night?"

Mayor Held turned his head pointedly toward Kari, and Roza followed his gaze.

"Oh, dear Sava." Her hand came up to her chest. "What's she doing here?"

"She wants her baby back."

"Send her away!" Roza said, her hand flicking toward Kari like she was shooing away a fly. "Kill her, if you want. I certainly won't be troubled with her any longer."

"I see. I suppose you made more money selling her child than you'd make in years of selling her," the mayor said.

Roza squared her shoulders. "You paid willingly."

"That I did."

"Why am I here, Mayor?"

"This woman broke into my house." For the first time that night, true anger gave substance to the mayor's words. "She stole my son from his bed and nearly ran out of the house with him. In the process, she woke my wife, who will have questions, and my servants, who will gossip until they're convinced they have answers. And that's all your problem, Roza. Not mine. You can't control your merchandise. What are you going to do about it?"

Roza's confidence at last faltered. She turned away from the mayor and paced a few steps before returning her gaze to his. "Can't you kill her?"

He released a loud sigh. "I'd rather avoid such a scandal. Right now, I'm a benevolent mayor who's given an orphan child a home. Let's not muddy that up with murder if we can avoid it."

Roza met his gaze again, and they stared at each other for several seconds. Then she turned away, pulled another upholstered chair right in front of Kari, and sat in it. Scorn caked her expression and thickened her voice. "I can't believe you came here."

Kari sat up straighter, holding Savala tight. "You can't believe I'd come rescue my son? Do you know anything about what it means to love, Roza?"

"I know more about love than you ever will."

Kari couldn't help it; she laughed.

Roza's jaw muscles tensed as she leaned toward Kari. "If you understood anything about love, you'd have thanked Yolin for taking your child. You'd have thanked the mayor, because he's giving your baby what you never can. Stability. A home steeped in moral tradition." She placed a hand on Savala's head, bringing her face even closer to Kari's.

"Kari, you killed your mother. Someone with more rational instincts could have saved her, but you walked off and left her to die."

How does she know that? Then Kari remembered the day she'd told Mara her whole story. Later they'd found out one of the other women of the house had been listening. Mara would never have shared, but the other woman would have.

Roza wasn't done. "Then you left your siblings. Where do you think they are now, Kari? How many starved or froze to death with no one to care for them? How many died of broken hearts when their oldest sister abandoned them?"

It wasn't until Roza reached up and wiped Kari's cheek that Kari realized she was crying.

"Oh, child," Roza said. "Your only skill is pleasing a man, and you weren't even very good at that. How is that knowledge going to help your son? What were you planning to do, work the streets at night, hoping he never found out what you were doing? They always find out, Kari. Always. And it breaks their hearts. That's why the women of Esherin House can't keep their babies. Because children deserve to grow up with mothers they can be proud of. Not mothers like you."

Kari was sobbing now, all her fears given substance in Roza's words, all the things she knew to be true about herself but was trying to forget. She managed to blurt out, "This is not a moral home."

Confusion twisted Roza's brow. "You mean because the mayor visits women like you? Kari, men have needs. He simply pays to get those needs met before returning to a life of serving our community." She laughed, the sound startling Kari. "I suppose you had a life of service too, but not the kind you can be proud of."

Kari shook her head and took several deep breaths, controlling her crying enough to say, "I don't want him raising my son. He's cruel."

"What did you say?" Mayor Held's voice boomed at Kari, and he took several steps toward her, until Roza lifted a hand, stopping him.

"Let me handle this," Roza said.

The mayor stepped away.

"The mayor is far too busy to spend much time with his son," Roza told Kari. "His wife, on the other hand, is kind and loving." She leaned close and whispered, "Much nicer than her husband, between you and me."

Leaning back again, Roza said, "Mrs. Held has dreamed for years of being a mother. She'll educate her new son to the highest standard.

She'll teach him about Sava, something you're certainly not qualified to do." Her voice grew hard. "You'd make a terrible mother, Kari."

Kari continued to hold her sleeping son close as she shook her head hard, trying to recapture her determination from earlier in the night. It was no use, though; Roza's words repeated in her head. *You killed your mother. You left your siblings. You'd make a terrible mother.* Moans emerged from her chest, but they weren't loud enough to drown out the terrible truth.

"Give me the baby," Roza said. "I'll bring him to his mother—his true mother, the one who can love him best. She'll tell him that the woman who gave birth to him cared enough to find a good home for him. Then you can leave, Kari. Find a new home. Do whatever you want. I won't even send Yolin after you.

"But if you don't leave on your own, Kari, we'll kill you. I don't care about the mayor's qualms. I'll kill you myself, and when this child gets old enough, Mayor Held will tell him his mother left him because she didn't love him. That's what he'll grow up believing."

"No!" Kari's voice was strained as she thrust each word at Roza. "Don't tell him that! It's not true!"

Roza placed both hands on Savala's tiny body. "Then give me the baby. You know it's the only right thing to do."

"No, please—"

"The only right thing, Kari! Give him to me!"

Kari cried out once, twice—and when her voice raised a third time, her arms, worn out by the weight of Roza's words, by years of knowing her own worthlessness, released her son.

Roza took him, and Kari stood, sobs shaking her entire body. She tried to tell Savala how sorry she was, but the words wouldn't form in her shaking throat.

She ran out the door, down the stairs, and into the night.

CHAPTER SEVEN

Alena turned her head first, and when she did, her thin legs halted their mad retreat. Alaya followed suit, and both children gazed on a sight like no other.

The bear stood tall, batting her paws around her, yet her sharp claws repeatedly hit an unseen barrier, and she cried in pitiful pain.

The children approached, and the bear again roared, but she could not touch them.

-from The Origin of Wild Magic *by Edoren the Bard*

KARI RAN THROUGH THE YARD, skirting wide around the stable. If she stopped there, Rusk would help her. But if he saw her without Savala, she'd have to tell him why she was leaving without her baby. She couldn't do that. Let him believe what he would; anything he could imagine would be preferable to the truth.

When she reached the trees, she ran until the mayor's land was out of sight. Then she fell to her knees and wept.

Every muscle in her body wanted to sprint back to the house and fight to the death for her son. But the truths Roza had thrown at her—she was a murderer, not a mother—multiplied in her mind, creating an unscalable wall between her and the big house.

I can't go back. I have to let go.

Certain her heart would collapse from the weight of her grief, she dug her fingers into the dirt beneath her. This would be her grave. She couldn't survive any more; surely her body knew that.

She lay down and closed her eyes, surrendering to the end.

THE SUN SHONE directly overhead when Kari woke.

No, no, no. She closed her eyes. She didn't want to wake up. Not now, not ever. Three years of misery was enough. Why didn't her body recognize that?

But she felt rested and healthy, sensations that mocked her broken heart.

Well, she felt healthy except for her chest, which was inexplicably sore. She pushed herself up to relieve the pressure of laying on her side, then touched her bodice. Her breasts were swollen and hard, and her dress was wet.

My milk. Of course. She'd seen her mother go through this over and over. A couple of days after a baby came, her mother's body began producing quantities of milk large enough to feed every infant in town.

My milk. For my baby. Kari dwelled on that truth.

Roza's words taunted her. *Killed your mother. Abandoned your siblings.*

"My milk," Kari said, her voice surprisingly strong. "For my baby."

Roza claimed Kari would be a terrible mother, but Kari's full breasts reminded her she was made to care for her child.

Yes, she'd left her family. But since then, she'd cared for pregnant women with a gentleness she didn't know she was capable of. She'd lived in the forest for months, nurturing the life in her. She'd given birth alone under a tree, in unthinkable pain, and never once regretted it. Because she loved her son.

She'd spent three years convincing herself she didn't know how to love others. And she'd spent those same three years proving otherwise. *Why didn't I see it until now?* Even her breasts, full of nourishment, screamed the truth. *I am capable of caring for my child!*

Roza's accusation of abandonment attempted to intrude into Kari's thoughts, but she drowned it out with a cry. "I won't abandon my son!"

She didn't know how she would take care of him, but she'd figure it out, just as she'd figured out how to survive every day since arriving in Esherin.

She had to get Savala back. An idea entered her mind, fully formed and brilliant enough to make her smile. Mara would need to help, and Kari knew her friend would say yes.

But there were a couple of things to take care of before she could go into the city. Kari could tell the rags Rusk had given her were nearing the end of their usefulness. She took off his cloak and used her teeth to break the thread at its hem. Then she tore off a long strip of it and used it as a rag. It wasn't what Rusk had given her the garment for, but she didn't think he'd mind.

That done, she ripped off a second strip and stuffed it in her bodice to soak up the leaking milk.

With an energy she hadn't felt since her labor started, Kari descended the hill.

KARI RETURNED to the forest where she'd spent her pregnancy. Once again, she had to wait until the middle of the night to approach Mara.

The delay was torturous in more than one way. The worst part was that every hour waiting was an hour away from Savala. On top of that, her breasts begged for relief. She expressed milk onto the forest floor, but she was still painfully full. Kari imagined the wet nurse, old and haggard with a wart on her nose, feeding Savala. She knew the picture couldn't be accurate, but it seemed natural to cast the woman as a villain.

Hours passed, and the sun set. After her long morning nap, Kari was wide awake. She sat, then paced, then tore off more of the fabric from Rusk's cloak. (Her mother had always bemoaned her bleeding and leaking breasts after childbirth, and Kari had never understood her better.) Eventually, she walked to the river for a drink of water. Hunger returned with a vengeance, but she ignored it.

At last, when she knew most of the city would be asleep, she left the forest and returned to the brothel.

This time, she stacked the crates first, trying to block out the sounds of Mara and the others servicing clients. As soon as the last man left, Kari climbed onto the first level of the shaky wooden staircase and tossed a few pebbles in the room.

Mara came to the window.

"Can you come down again?"

Mara descended more confidently than she had two nights before. They walked back to their spot outside the closed pub.

As Kari shared her idea, she couldn't see Mara's face well enough to gauge her friend's reaction. She finished and waited in anxious silence.

Mara's arms came around Kari and squeezed tight enough for Kari to yelp.

Pulling away, Mara asked, "Are you all right?"

"My milk came in."

"Oh, you dear girl." Mara hugged her again, this time more gently, and whispered in Kari's ear. "Leave it to you to come up with a plan that helps me as much as it helps you. You're the best person I know, Kari."

Kari was sick of crying, but she couldn't stop herself this time.

Mara held her, and when Kari had calmed down, Mara said, "I know one more person who will want to help us."

Kari pulled away. "Who?"

"You'll see." Mara stood and held out her hand. "Come on. We're going there now."

"It's the middle of the night!"

"Come on!"

Kari sighed and followed Mara. They jumped over the sewer trench and made their way between two houses, emerging onto the street behind the brothel.

When they stopped, Kari looked at the house before them. Suspicion flooded her mind. "I can't tell in the dark," she murmured. "What color is this house?"

"Blue."

Kari grabbed Mara's arm. "I don't want to see Dom!"

"He asks about you all the time! He'll kill me if I don't bring him in on this!"

"But of all people—" She gestured down at herself. Even in the dark, she was all too aware of the fabric stuffed awkwardly in her bodice, her rounded abdomen, and the insect bites on her face. "I don't want him to see me like this."

Mara spun and brought her face close enough for Kari to make out her features. "Your plan is good. But Dom will make it better. And trust me, he won't care what you look like; he'll just be glad to see you."

She didn't wait for a response, walking right up to the front porch. Kari reluctantly followed.

A minute or so later, Dom himself was at the door, dressed in a nightshirt and trousers, carrying a candle with one hand and rubbing his eyes with the other. "Mara?" Then his gaze shifted to the left. His eyes widened, and a smile filled his entire face. "Kari!"

"Dom, come with us," Mara said. "We need your help."

He all but leapt out of the house and onto the porch.

"You can put on a regular shirt and some shoes first," Mara said.

With an embarrassed chuckle, Dom went back inside.

Soon, the three of them sat next to the abandoned pub. Dom set his candleholder in the dirt at their feet, then smiled at Kari. "Nice boots."

She almost told him about the boots appearing magically, but he might think she was crazy. Instead, she said, "Thanks."

After a pause, he spoke again, his voice soft. "My mom was so confused when I told her I needed her new boots. When she found out why, she was happy to give them to me."

Kari stopped breathing. She stared at Dom. "You brought me the boots? And the other things too?"

"Yes. I told Yolin I'd come with him to search for you. I was hoping to find you myself and keep him away. It didn't quite work out." He paused, then said, "I'm glad you got away from him, Kari. When we were coming back here, he told me to carry your dress, and I dropped it on the path. Did you find it?"

"Yes."

"Good. I came back that night. I was hoping to bring you to my house; my mother said you could stay there. I brought the boots and things in case you wouldn't come. But I couldn't find you. So I left the boots. I kept coming back, at least once a week, looking for you. I even saw you sometimes, from far away. But for some reason, I could never get to you."

Kari didn't respond. It seemed that in the forest, magic had blocked both her enemy and her friend from reaching her.

"Kari, what can I do to help you?" Dom asked. "Do you need a safe place to have your baby?"

Kari's hand covered her middle, and her breath caught as the reality of Savala's absence again sliced at her heart. She wished it were daytime, so Dom could see that her pregnancy was over and her son wasn't in her arms. She couldn't bring herself to disclose the terrible truth.

Mara spoke instead, explaining in a voice of soft determination why they needed Dom's help.

When she finished, Dom's warm hand found Kari's. His voice was strangely choked. "I knew Yolin was chasing you. I tried to follow him whenever I could. But I think he saw me a couple of times, and he started leaving at all hours, sneaking away when he knew I was sleeping or on a job. Oh, Kari, I'm sorry."

She was crying. Again. "Why did you try to help me?"

"Because you're my friend."

Kari reached out and put her arms around him, burying her face in his shirt. He responded, his own strong arms encircling her, squeezing tightly. It hurt her aching chest, but she didn't mind.

Mara cleared her throat, and Kari pulled away. "I'm sorry, Dom." She brushed at his shirt, where her tears had dampened the fabric.

"Kari," Dom said, "we're friends, remember? Hug me any time you want."

"This is all very sweet," Mara said, her dry tone the perfect remedy for Kari's tears. "But the mayor has Kari's baby, and we have a plan to get him back. Dom, will you help us?"

"I'll do anything I can."

And Kari believed him.

HALF AN HOUR LATER, Kari climbed up the crates. It was more nerve-racking than she'd expected. "You're sure these will hold?" she asked Mara, who'd already gone up.

Mara shrugged. "They held for me."

Kari made it inside and waved out the window to Dom, who began moving the crates away from the house.

Mara gestured to the bed. "Sleep there. I'll keep watch and talk to the others."

"You need to sleep, too."

"I'll be fine. I remember what it's like after giving birth. Sleep for a few hours, and then . . . it'll be time." In the dim candlelight, Mara's eyes gleamed.

KARI WAS awake when Mara came into the room not long after dawn.

"Let's go," Mara said.

Kari stretched. "How many are coming with us?"

"Six—plus you, me, and Dom."

Kari smiled. Ten women worked at Esherin House. Seven of them together could make a big difference—in their own lives and Kari's.

When Kari and Mara entered the hallway, the six other women were waiting, all carrying lit candles. They smiled at their old housemate.

The women descended the stairs quietly and walked through the center hallway. Kari swung the front door open, and Dom entered, grinning at her.

The group crept down a side hallway. Standing in front of a thick, oak door, they exchanged nervous glances. None of them had ever dared enter Roza and Yolin's room. Until today.

Mara pushed down on the latch, and the door swung open.

The shutters were closed, but the group's candles lit up the room, illuminating two figures in bed.

Roza and Yolin were already awake. Yolin was sitting on the edge of the bed, pulling his trousers on. Doubtless, they'd heard the front door open when Dom had entered.

"What is this?" Roza's voice was both sleepy and shrill. "Get out of our room!"

"Stay right where you are," Mara said. "We're here to talk to both of you."

Two of the women had gone straight to the room's two windows, and the area filled with dawn light as they pushed the shutters open.

Roza crossed her arms over her thin gown. "You do not make the rules around here!"

"We do now." Mara's voice was firm and loud.

Roza turned to the bleary-eyed man next to her. "Stop them, Yolin!"

"But there's"—he halted, counting the women—"eight of them!"

"Stop them!"

"I can't!"

"He's right; he can't stop us," Mara said. "Neither of you can. I suggest you shut your mouths and listen."

"At least let me put a robe over my nightclothes," Roza said.

The entire group stared at her. Finally, Mara spoke. "That's the last thing you deserve. But today is the day we bring respect to this house. You may put on your robe."

Roza got out of bed and pulled her robe off a hook on the wall, covering her lightweight nightclothes. Her gaze darted from one woman to another.

"Make yourselves comfortable, by all means," Mara said.

The owner of Esherin House and her husband sat in two upholstered chairs on either side of a low tea table.

"What's this all about?" Roza asked.

"Remember?" Mara said. "It's my turn to talk, not yours."

Roza's mouth levered shut.

Mara stood up straight and squared her shoulders. "Starting today, you will treat the women of this house with dignity and respect," Mara said. "I'll give you several conditions. You may agree to all of them, and we will stay here. Or you may refuse any of them, and we will leave your employment. You will be left with three women, and we all know the three that aren't standing here are the three who bring in the least income."

Kari hadn't actually known that, but it didn't surprise her. The three women Mara referred to were loyal to Roza and mirrored her bitter disposition.

Mara continued, "You will pay all of us, every week, half the income we bring in."

Roza blanched.

"It shouldn't be difficult, since you've been saving up all that money for us for years," Mara said, her gaze drilling into Roza's. "We aren't even asking for back pay, though you owe it to us. However, we don't trust your ability to keep honest records. I will now be in charge of the accounts of the house. I will work with you to make sure every coin is accounted for and every woman gets her due. We will also raise prices, which will allow us to be more selective in which clients we accept."

Kari wished she could cheer. Mara's bearing was regal, and she'd never looked stronger. Kari realized, however, that she'd seen hints of this confidence ever since Mara's child had been taken. Grief had somehow forged Mara into a tougher, shrewder version of herself, a woman who wouldn't be controlled even by a master manipulator.

Mara wasn't done. "Roza, you will receive a salary from the house profits. This salary will be contingent on you protecting the women of the house from anyone who might hurt us, including Yolin. If you fail to protect us, we will run your business into the ground."

Roza's chin was hanging lower than Kari had ever seen it. At last, she brought her lips back together, licked them, and croaked, "I do not agree with your ridiculous terms."

Mara ignored the statement. She gestured to one of the younger women. "Alia hates her work here. She will no longer entertain men at night. Instead, we will create a welcoming tea house downstairs. She will serve tea and sweets every afternoon and evening to our male customers and anyone else who visits. We are confident this will further increase our profits."

Roza opened her mouth to argue, but Mara's hand snapped up, and the madam swallowed and sat back.

"As of right now, the rest of us want to keep our current positions," Mara said.

Kari looked down. She wanted the other women to be free from this place. But Mara insisted she knew no other life. Apparently all of the others except Alia had agreed.

Mara wasn't done. "But if any of us wants to help Alia in the tea house, you'll allow it. And if anyone wants to leave, you'll allow that, too. Kari, as I'm sure you've guessed, is not returning."

"But she—" Roza said.

For the first time, Dom spoke. "She's not returning."

Kari put a firm hand on Dom's arm. She needed to speak for herself. Taking a step forward, she said, "You couldn't say anything to get me back here, Roza. And you're going with us to the mayor's house today to get my baby back."

Roza stood and strode right up to Kari. "I will do no such thing. You're a terrible mother. I couldn't in good conscience allow a baby to stay with you."

Kari opened her mouth, but Roza's statements had taken on substance, wrapping around Kari's throat, preventing both words and breath from emerging.

Dom stepped up next to Kari. But he didn't look at her, reserving his searing gaze for Roza. "You're lying to her because you don't want to lose the money you made selling her son." His voice was quiet, but deep and unshakable, the voice of a man. "Kari has everything she needs to be a good mother. She loves her son. She's committed to him.

"And although she could raise him on her own, she shouldn't have to. I'll help her, if she'll let me. My mother will help. We'll bring the entire community around her if she needs it. He'll be the best-cared-for child in the city, if I have anything to say about it."

Kari gaped at Dom. Her breath returned. *I can do this.* The thought buried itself in her heart, and, to her surprise, she believed it. *I can do this.* She wanted to break down in tears and thank Dom, but it wasn't the time for that. Instead, she reached her hand down and found his waiting.

He gripped her hand and finally looked at her, giving her a small smile before looking back at Roza. His expression turned firm again. "I didn't know until today that you've been selling babies. Roza, you'll agree to all the terms Mara stated, but that's not all. You'll also talk to every woman here who's had a baby. You'll help them establish any communication they desire with their children and their new families."

Roza took a step back. "I certainly will not—"

"If you don't follow through on any of this," Dom said, "I'll tell my father exactly what's been happening here. He'll arrest you and Yolin. What do you think a trial will do to your livelihood?"

Kari almost laughed as Roza's and Yolin's jaws dropped.

"I—I haven't agreed to any of this," Roza said, her voice loud but wavering. "Nor will I."

Mara strode all the way up to Roza, standing close enough that the madam again stepped back. "The other women and I considered leaving this morning," Mara said, her voice low. "I have multiple wealthy clients I'm confident would invest in a new brothel staffed by skilled women. We are willing to stay because Esherin House is already an established, successful business. But if you prefer we leave so this place turns into a laughingstock while you two defend your-selves in court, just say the word."

Roza's eyes were so full of venom, Kari wondered that her gaze didn't burn through them all. But Mara stood her ground, waiting in silent dignity for Roza's response.

At last, Roza's mouth opened just far enough for her to spit out a command. "Yolin, get the carriage ready for a trip to the mayor's house."

Kari squeezed Dom's hand. Mara looked back at them both, her dark brows raised in victory. It was time for the women of Esherin House to be treated with dignity.

And it was time for Kari to get her son back.

CHAPTER EIGHT

*A crowd gathered, and a man handed Alaya a club carved from a thick branch.
Though the weapon was large, the boy swung it at the bear, once, twice, thrice,
knocking the great beast to the ground. He finished her with further strikes,
for she could not escape her mysterious cage.*

*The community ate bear stew that night and held a celebration like no other.
They knew not what had stopped the bear, but the same force returned to the
world in coming days. Sick children became well, crops grew out of season,
and a cooking fire burned through a rainstorm.*

This magic, *as they called it, was unpredictable, coming and going as it
pleased. Yet it granted some the gift of survival, preventing humanity's
demise.*

*In time, people sought to know the one who created magic. Throughout the
world, this one is given many names and is worshipped in countless ways. In
our land, he is known as Sava, our rescuer, our god.*

-from The Origin of Wild Magic *by Edoren the Bard*

ROZA'S CARRIAGE was only big enough for four passengers. Yolin drove, and Roza, Kari, Mara, and Dom rode in the back. Kari didn't like being in enclosed quarters with Roza, but it helped to have a friend by her side and another in the seat across from her.

Two friends. The very idea was implausible, but there they were. All she needed was Savala in her arms, and her life would be more perfect than she'd ever dared to hope.

It was a quiet trip, and Kari didn't mind the silence. Roza's face was stuck in a puckered position like she was holding a fresh lemon wedge between her teeth.

When the carriage reached the top of the hill (a much easier trip with two horses and four wheels), Kari took a deep, slow breath. Mayor Held was the last person she wanted to see, but Roza had agreed to the terms given to her by the women and Dom. Surely the visit would be short.

They pulled up to the front of the big house, disembarked, and walked to the door. Kari felt sure her heart was louder than Yolin's knocking.

A maid came to the door. "Yes?"

Everyone looked at Roza, and after a short pause, she spoke as if the words were bile in her throat. "We need an audience with the mayor. Tell him it's Roza, and it's urgent."

"Yes, ma'am. Will you wait in the sitting room, please?"

"We will."

"Shall I have the groom take your carriage to the back?"

"No need. We won't be long."

The maid nodded and led them to the sitting room, then hurried off.

As soon as they entered the room, Kari doubted her decision to remove her son from this place. Everything was luxurious—fabrics, curtains, polished wooden floors. Even the candles glowing in wall sconces looked smoother and whiter than any candle she'd ever used. *Any child growing up here would have everything they need.*

Mayor Held entered. He looked straight at Kari and sneered at her.

And any child growing up here would have to deal with him. Kari smiled at him, her doubts allayed.

Mayor Held sat in a tall chair near the fire. Its padded upholstery looked impossibly soft. He didn't say a word until he had situated himself. At last, he said, "What can I do for you . . . ladies . . . and gentlemen?" He made *ladies* sound like a profanity.

Kari looked to Roza, but it was Mara who spoke first. "We'll have a seat," she said, her jaw squared and gaze bold.

She sat in the chair nearest the mayor. Kari followed suit, settling herself on a small sofa. Dom sat with her. Only Roza and Yolin didn't move, instead gazing at the mayor with uncertain expressions. Mayor Held said nothing, and the madam and her husband remained standing.

"Roza has something to tell you," Mara said.

All eyes turned to Roza. She licked her lips, swallowed, and said, "Mayor Held, I'm sorry—terribly sorry, really—but we—we'll need the baby back."

Gazes returned to the mayor, who still sat calmly, elbows on the armrests of his chair, fingers steepled in front of his mouth. His arrogant expression didn't change. "I have no idea what baby you're referring to."

Kari's breaths quickened.

"Kari's baby!" Roza snapped. "I brought the money with me; you'll get it all back. I'm sorry it didn't work out, but we need him back."

Mayor Held stared at Roza, finally speaking one word: "Money?"

She nodded several times as she approached him, holding out a velvet coin purse that jingled as she walked. "It's all here."

He accepted the purse, opened it, and gave the interior a cursory glance before returning his attention to Roza. His pale eyebrows rose. "I'm sure we all agree children must be with their parents. One moment, please."

Kari didn't take her eyes off him as he walked to the door, beckoned the same maid who'd let them in, whispered in her ear, and returned to his seat.

"This shouldn't take long," he said, addressing the words to Kari.

Kari swallowed and nodded, then turned and watched the door.

She didn't trust the mayor's motives for a second, but thank Sava the man wasn't putting up a fight. Perhaps he was tired of listening to a baby cry. Perhaps he regretted giving up so much money. *He's returning your son, Kari. It doesn't matter why.*

Her breasts throbbed in time to her rapid heartbeat, and she blinked hard, refusing her emotions the release they demanded. When Savala came, she'd take him in her arms and walk out that front door with her head held high, saving the tears for when they were alone.

Footsteps sounded in the hall, and Kari curled her toes to prevent herself from running to the door. After a wait that felt interminable, the maid appeared.

But there was no baby in her arms, only several loose papers. From where he sat, Mayor Held extended a hand. The maid walked in and gave him the papers. He spent at least a minute looking through them. The sound of Kari's breaths filled the room, accented only by the shuffle of fine paper.

At last, the mayor spoke. "As I said, children should be with their parents. And when a child has no parents, people of principle must step up and remedy such a tragedy. Recently, a citizen went into the woods and found a baby boy abandoned by its heartless mother." Mayor Held's eyes found Kari as he spoke those words. "My wife and I gave him a home. We are his parents. I have here the adoption papers, signed by a judge."

The only sound was the distant caw of a crow.

At last, Roza asked, "Papers?"

"Of course." He held them up. "We'd certainly never adopt a child without papers."

Kari had no doubt Mayor Held had the connections to get whatever papers he needed. She drew in a single breath, and when she exhaled, a high moan emerged.

Mayor Held shook the coin purse and returned his gaze to Roza. "I suppose you'll want this back. I'm not sure why you were under the impression it came from me."

Roza's eyes darted from the mayor to Dom to Yolin. She grabbed the purse and shoved it in her dress pocket.

The mayor's eyes found Kari's, and his bearded cheeks widened into a smile, if such an unfriendly expression could be called that.

She was certain he'd taken that purse only to keep her hope alive. She swallowed, this time to keep herself from vomiting.

Yolin advanced to the mayor, standing over him. His voice carried in the quiet room. "Mayor, for years, we've been finding good homes for the babies born in our care. But now if that little"—his blue eyes narrowed at Kari before turning back to the mayor—"if that *young lady* there doesn't get her baby back, Dom here says his father will arrest me and Roza."

"How terrible." Mayor Held's tone was infuriatingly nonchalant. "Step away from me, Yolin."

Yolin obeyed.

"Mayor."

It was Dom this time, and the mayor's eyes lazily turned his way.

"I don't think you understand," Dom said. "Whatever those papers say, all of us will testify that the baby is Kari's. My father will arrest you, too."

"Oh, really?" The mayor sat up straighter. "You saw her give birth, did you? Or perhaps met the baby afterward?"

Dom hesitated, then said more quietly, "Yolin saw her with the baby." His pleading eyes shifted to Yolin.

"Hmm." Mayor Held smiled at Yolin, then at Roza. "The permit to continue running your fine establishment is up for renewal soon. I'm looking forward to approving it. What was it you saw, Yolin?"

Yolin glanced at Kari, then pulled his eyes back to the mayor. He made a show of shrugging. "Didn't see nothing."

Wringing her hands, Roza turned to Yolin. "But our girls—Mara they said they'll leave."

Yolin folded his arms. "They won't. What are they gonna do if they leave? Mayor Held won't let them start their own place, right, Mayor?"

Mayor Held pointed at Mara. "Run by her? Certainly not." He smirked, then turned toward Dom, eyes narrowing. "You're quite an idealistic young man, aren't you? I think you've forgotten I'm the one who appointed your father to his position, and I can remove him at any time. For any reason. Now, if there's nothing else, I'll ask you all to kindly leave." He stood, and his pale lips twitched into a dangerous smile as his eyes turned to Mara. "I look forward to seeing you soon."

Kari's aching chest was rising and falling far too quickly. The mayor's triumph was mirrored on Yolin's face, though Roza's nervous gaze still rested on Mara. Dom and Mara each held one of Kari's hands, and they appeared as helpless as she felt.

Roza and Yolin ushered the group toward the door.

"What do we do?" Mara whispered.

"I don't know," Dom replied.

They were in the entryway, though Kari wasn't sure how they'd gotten there. Surely she hadn't willfully moved her feet toward the front door? She looked to her right at a massive set of stairs with polished, wooden steps and banisters.

My son is up there.

Another step toward the exit.

My son is up there!

Kari yanked her hands away from Mara and Dom, summoned all her desperation into her booted feet, and ran.

"Stop!" Mayor Held shouted.

Scuffling sounded behind Kari, but she didn't have time to turn and see what was happening.

"Go, Kari! Go!" Mara screamed.

Oh, she was going. She grasped the smooth banister in her left hand and hiked up her skirt with her right. Two steps at a time, then three. The thick soles of her boots echoed on the wooden steps, announcing to all the world that she was a mother, and she wouldn't give up.

The scuffles below were louder now, but Kari was at the top of the stairs, and she darted down the hall, all the way to the nursery, throwing the door open.

Inside, the nurse (young, with no visible warts) gaped at Kari. But the crib was empty.

Racing footsteps sounded on the stairs.

With a guttural cry of fury, Kari darted to the next door. She slammed her hand down on the latch and pushed the door, but it didn't open.

Locked.

Then she saw it—a simple hook on the door, inserted in a metal ring on the frame. With a flick of her fingers, she loosed it, just as Mayor Held reached the top of the stairs.

Screaming, Kari pushed the door open, darted in the room, and slammed her back against the door, determined not to let the mayor in.

She didn't have time to scan the room before the door pressed against her back, accompanied by the loud *smack* of a fist or shoulder on the other side. Mayor Held was larger and stronger than her, but Kari had a mother's determination, and she'd die before letting him in this room. The door jarred her again.

Suddenly, a man was next to her, his red beard surrounding a determined mouth. *Rusk!* Again, the door shook, and it almost pushed Kari over. But Rusk's boot came up, pressing the bottom of the door nearly back into place.

"Push!" he said. "I need to lock it!"

Kari pushed with all her might as the door trembled again.

"It's locked!" Rusk said. "Let me stand here, Kari. I don't know how long the lock will keep him out."

Kari nodded and shifted to the side while Rusk took her place, standing against the still-shuddering door. Feet set wide apart, arms folded over a thick chest, he looked like some divine hero.

"You do what you need to do," he said, his voice just loud enough for Kari to hear.

She pulled her eyes away from him and took in the beautifully appointed bedroom. Mrs. Held stood by the window, jaw clenched, staring at Kari. Light brown hair, perfectly pinned up, sat over a face featuring wide eyes and a parted mouth.

And in her arms was a sleeping baby.

The pounding at the door continued, accompanied now by threats and curses in the mayor's voice. But all that faded as Kari walked slowly across the room, something telling her she needed to handle this woman carefully. At last, she reached Mrs. Held.

"I'm Kari." The words pushed past what must be a massive stone imbedded in her throat. "That's my son."

The skin between Mrs. Held's eyebrows compressed, harsh wrinkles appearing there. She held Savala tighter to her chest. "No, he was found in the woods. Abandoned. He's ours now."

"Mrs. Held." Rusk's voice rang from across the room, loud and firm, and Kari was again aware of the banging and the mayor's furious demands. "You know it's the truth," Rusk said. "It's the same thing I was telling you."

Kari looked at him, and a sob escaped her mouth. He'd come here to fight for her. For her son.

"No!" The mayor's wife insisted. "My husband told me the truth! This baby is ours! You must leave!"

When Kari turned back toward Mrs. Held, the woman's gaze was defiant, as immovable as her tight hands around the child she believed was hers. Crying in earnest now, Kari looked back at Rusk, silently begging him to speak when she could not.

"I know your husband told you some other story," he said, his voice filling the room above the pounding of the thick door. "Tell me, didn't he also lock this door when Kari got here, so you couldn't go downstairs and hear her out?"

Mrs. Held didn't answer. Keeping her rigid gaze on Kari, she turned her body to protect the baby in her arms.

Still weeping, Kari reached into the bodice of her dress and pulled out the rough canvas, torn from Rusk's cloak. It was wet and smelled of milk. She held it out to the mayor's wife.

"What's that?" Mrs. Held asked, but her expression told Kari that she already knew the answer.

Kari managed one word through her sobs: "Milk."

As if on cue, Savala began to squirm in Mrs. Held's arms. A few perfect, little grunts emerged from him, and then his tiny mouth opened wide, and he began crying as hard as his mother.

Mrs. Held shushed the child in a surprisingly gentle voice, swaying with him, but Savala cried harder.

Kari held out her arms. "He's hungry. Please, let me feed him."

Mrs. Held ignored her, continuing to attempt to soothe the baby. His crying didn't abate.

"Please." Kari could barely speak through her tears. Her breasts competed with her heart to see which could ache the most. "I just want to feed him."

At last, the mayor's wife turned to Kari. "He needs to eat." She glared at the door, which was still shuddering every time the mayor pounded it. Rusk still stood there, not only preventing Mayor Held from getting in, but also preventing Mrs. Held from exiting. "I can't get his nurse." Her eyes burned into Kari's. "You'll have to do, just this once." She pulled Savala away from her own chest and placed the screaming baby in his mother's arms.

Kari tried to thank her, but her uncontrolled sobs wouldn't allow it. She held Savala tight and walked to a chair by the fireplace. Heedless of the others in the room, she unbuttoned her bodice and brought her child's screaming mouth to her breast. He eagerly latched on, then looked up at her. Savala stopped crying, and Kari followed suit, captivated by the intelligent gaze of his dark eyes.

A new noise thrust itself into the room—the distinct *crack* of wood.

"The lock's breaking!" Rusk said.

"Let him in." Mrs. Held's voice was calm and clear.

"No," Rusk said, and he turned around, bracing one foot behind the other and pressing his arms against the shaking door.

But it wasn't enough. With another great *crack*, the doorframe broke, and the door itself pushed open, toppling Rusk onto the floor. He hurled himself back at the door, but not quickly enough. Mayor Held was already in the room.

The mayor glared down at him. "You really thought you could keep me out? I had help. Most of my staff are loyal. Get out of here, Rusk."

"No," Mrs. Held said. "He's staying."

Several quick, long strides brought the mayor to his wife. He stood over her. "What did you say?"

"I said he's staying. When you're in a mood like this, I want another man in the room."

Mayor Held looked like he'd respond, but then his gaze found Kari. His head swiveled back toward his wife. He grasped both her shoulders in his hands, and she winced.

"Why is that woman feeding our son?" His voice was dangerously low.

Mrs. Held squirmed, trying to evade his grasp, but his grip was unrelenting. Before long, she released her breath and stopped fighting. Anger warped every plane of her face. "He was screaming. Surely you heard him."

At last, the mayor released his wife's shoulders. She brought both hands up to rub the soreness out as her husband strode to Kari. He sneered at her, even as he spoke to his wife. "If you had any idea what kind of woman this is, you wouldn't allow her to touch your child."

Kari glared at him, then pulled her gaze back down to Savala, who was eating peacefully, his suckling slowing as his eyes fought to stay awake.

"I do know who she is," Mrs. Held said.

Kari's head snapped up, and she found the mayor's wife's gaze waiting.

"Rusk guessed she came from the brothel," Mrs. Held said, disgust thick in her voice. "based on her dress and their conversations."

As soon as she heard Rusk's name, Kari turned toward him, expecting to see judgment in his gaze. Instead, he watched her with his head tilted. When their eyes met, his mouth curved into a gentle smile.

"And you're letting her feed our son?" The mayor's voice was loud enough now that Kari moved a hand to cover her child's ear.

"He's not ours!" Mrs. Held took several steps toward her husband, though she stopped before she was within his reach. She whispered, but the words were clear in the silent room. "Why did you let her in here? Why didn't you let me keep believing he was abandoned?"

"Who cares who gave birth to him?" The mayor was still shouting. "He's ours now, legally. He's certainly not leaving here with some prostitute."

"I don't work there anymore," Kari said, the volume of her voice surprising her. She cleared her throat. "And I have friends who will help me give my son a good life."

"Yes," Rusk said. "I'm one of them."

Kari swallowed. Rusk didn't even know her. She couldn't fathom where his kindness came from, but she nodded to him in gratitude.

Mayor Held stood up straight, crossing his arms. The look in his eyes made Kari glad Rusk was in the room. The mayor looked capable of murder. "He's our son!" Then, in a flash, he was leaning over Kari. He grabbed Savala and pulled hard, screaming, "Hand him over!"

Savala's drowsiness fled, his mouth releasing his mother's nipple. He wailed again. Kari held him tight, but Mayor Held just pulled harder. Her child's desperate, frightened screams rending her heart, Kari twisted, trying unsuccessfully to release her son from the mayor's grip.

Suddenly, the mayor stopped pulling Savala. Relief flooded Kari until Mayor Held's hands shoved past her arms, one grasping the baby's head, one gripping his tiny neck.

"I can break his neck," the mayor said, his voice deathly quiet, "or you can hand him over."

Kari didn't hesitate. Her hands and arms relaxed, even as a cry of anguish exploded out of her throat.

Mayor Held took her child in his big hands, then held Savala's screaming form out to his wife. "Take him," he demanded. "I'll get his nurse."

But Mrs. Held's hands were at her side, and she didn't lift them. Instead, she stared at her husband, her breaths coming rapidly.

"Take him!" The mayor shoved the squalling child toward his wife, who complied, pulling Savala to her chest.

Without a word, the mayor turned and walked toward the door.

His wife's voice stopped him. "Wait."

He turned, and when she said nothing else, he thrust his arms out to either side. "What is it, woman?"

Moving slowly, this time Mrs. Held stepped close enough for her husband to touch her. Screaming baby between them, she lifted her chin and met his gaze, her eyes as fiery as his. "Do you really think I can look at this child now, knowing his mother didn't abandon him, and be happy to hold him? You must be an idiot! I can't forget what I know to be true!"

"You must be an idiot not to take a child who's legally yours because some girl barely out of diapers herself claims to be his mother!" Mayor Held took a step back. "Can you please shut that baby up?"

"No!" Mrs. Held said with a wild laugh. "But she can!" She stepped to Kari and thrust Savala back in her arms. Kari brought him to her breast, and he latched on, his wails again subsiding.

"Take him back!" Mayor Held said. "He's ours!"

The mayor's wife stared at Savala for several seconds, and behind the woman's anger, Kari saw heartbreak. Finally, Mrs. Held turned back to her husband. "Then you can raise him by yourself, because this isn't adoption, it's theft. I'm not living every day of my life wondering if Sava will curse me for stealing a child."

The mayor laughed. "You'd never leave me. Where are you going to go, back home to your parents' hovel?"

His wife didn't flinch. "Yes. And on my way out of town, I'll tell all your secrets to anyone who will listen. We'll start with your visits to the brothel. How's that for a scandal? Elections are coming up in a few months. I guess you'll need to find a new home, too. Can't live in the mayor's house if you're not the mayor anymore."

Kari watched the exchange. She'd assumed Mayor Held had his wife under his thumb, and in some ways, that was true. The man had a lock on the outside of her door, after all.

But Mrs. Held was no delicate hummingbird. She was as strong as her husband in her own way. Clearly, they'd arranged a relationship that worked for both of them, based not on love or respect, but on mutual benefit.

What a terrible way to live. Kari held Savala tighter. She couldn't get him away from these people soon enough.

Whatever the nature of the silent negotiation happening in front of Kari, it was clear the moment it ended. Both the mayor and his wife nodded once, and the mayor turned to Kari. "Get out of my house. You and your brat."

Savala had drifted to sleep, and as Kari gently pulled him off her breast and buttoned her dress, the mayor turned to Rusk.

"You'd better find another job."

"He's staying," Mrs. Held said.

Kari watched the interchange, her gaze shifting to Rusk. Mrs. Held depended on him as one line of defense against her husband, and though Kari hadn't known Rusk for long, she'd already experienced his fierce protective nature. Yet she could also see the distaste on his face as he stared at Mayor Held. How long could he continue working for such an employer?

The mayor glared at his wife for a minute, then threw his hands up. "Fine, he's staying." He turned back to his groom. "But keep out of my business, and keep out of my house."

"I'll escort the lady downstairs," Rusk said.

"Oh yes," the mayor responded, "please do escort *the lady*." He threw Kari a look of thick contempt, then left the room. A moment later, a door slammed.

Kari stood with Savala and turned to Mrs. Held. "Thank you."

Mrs. Held folded her arms so tightly, she must have cut off her own circulation. Her eyes shone as she turned away and crossed to the window. "Go."

Just as Kari and Rusk were about to exit, Mayor Held strode up, blocking the doorway. His gaze could have burned the entire forest Kari had spent so many months in.

Kari froze, holding Savala tighter, dread flooding her entire body. "I don't care what you say. I'm taking my son."

"You stupid girl," Mayor Held stepped right up to her, close enough for her to see the rapid pulse in his neck. His low voice grated in her ears. "You should know I'm burning those adoption papers as soon as you leave. So don't dream of coming back here and claiming we owe your child anything."

Kari stared at him, resisting competing urges—to hit him, to hug him, to spit at him. Instead, she drew in a breath and spoke in a steady voice. "You're in our way." Relief washed over her as Mayor Held spun and strode out of the room.

Rusk led Kari downstairs. Roza, Yolin, Mara, and Dom all waited at the bottom of the steps. Several servants stood there, some of them holding kitchen knives, preventing the visitors from going upstairs.

"Pardon me," Kari said.

The servants turned to look at her but didn't move until Mrs. Held's tired voice called down the stairs, "Let them go."

The servants parted, and Kari walked toward the front door, head held high. She didn't look to either side, but in her peripheral vision, she saw Dom join her on one side and Mara on the other. Rusk held the front door open, catching Kari's eye as she approached. He flashed her a small smile.

Outside, the sun greeted them with warm rays, and Savala's eyes squeezed tighter shut. Kari held him to her chest, breathed in the perfect scent of his skin and hair, and christened him with her tears.

EPILOGUE

FOURTEEN YEARS LATER

"WELL DONE," Kari said.

The woman in the bed was flushed and sweaty, but she beamed at Kari, then returned her gaze to the newborn in her arms.

Kari smiled at her apprentice, who stood on the other side of the bed. "I think you can handle the afterbirth."

"By myself?"

"I'll just be a shout away if you need help. You can do this, Mara." Kari smiled at her old friend.

Mara had spent well over a decade leading the women of Esherin House, fighting for fair pay and dignity. Two years earlier, however, Mayor Held had finally left office, embroiled in a financial scandal. His replacement put laws in place to protect workers, including women at brothels. The authorities immediately began keeping a tight rein on Roza. Yolin had died years earlier, having succumbed to copious drinking after losing control of the brothel's women.

Knowing her friends were safe, Mara had left Esherin House. Now, as a midwife apprentice, she treated expectant mothers with a gentleness that couldn't be taught. She wasn't confident in her skills yet, but Kari was convinced Mara would make a fine midwife.

Kari still found it hard to believe that she had enough clients to take on an apprentice. Thirteen years earlier, when she had sought a local midwife to train her, only one had been willing—an older midwife who had long had a heart for the women of Esherin House.

At first, most of the midwife's clients refused to see a former prostitute. But one woman gave Kari a chance, then another. Tales of her kindness and skill spread. By the time her mentor retired, Kari had become one of the most respected midwives in the city.

Kari made her way through the midwife house, entering the half of the building she used as a residence. In the kitchen, she washed her hands then stood over the basin, eyes closed. She'd been up since her patient had arrived in the middle of the night. Now it was mid-afternoon. Bedtime couldn't come soon enough.

She looked up when she heard footsteps entering the room.

Jenki smiled. "I finally got her to sleep."

Kari nodded at her sister. "Oh, good." Kari's youngest had been up half the previous night, and for most of the day, she'd refused to nap.

"I think I'll lie down, too," Jenki said.

"Lucky you." Kari smiled and watched Jenki leave.

After getting her son back, Kari had returned to her hometown, accompanied by Dom, his mother, and of course Savala. There, she found that her siblings had indeed been adopted by townspeople. Not everyone was happy to see Kari, but Jenki, who was nearly an adult by then, couldn't have been more pleased to reconnect with her oldest sister. She'd returned to Esherin and lived with Kari ever since. Now she cared for Kari's three young children.

"Mother?"

Her sleepy reverie broken, Kari looked up and smiled at Savala, who stood in the kitchen's open doorway, barefoot. "Child, where are your shoes?"

"Well, that's what I wanted to talk to you about." Savala gave her that gentle smile of his. "Why don't we sit, Mother? You look tired."

"I am." Kari sat in one of the chairs at the kitchen table. "How was your riding lesson?"

Savala settled himself across from her. "Rusk says I'm almost as good as he is now." He laughed, and the deep tone of it made Kari flinch. Where had her little boy gone? "I'm pretty sure I don't need lessons anymore. I think he just likes having someone to ride with."

Joining in his laughter, Kari said, "You're probably right. His wife hates riding." When Rusk had married several years earlier, he'd left the mayor's employment and opened a stable in town, where he bred and trained horses. "Now—back to your lack of shoes?"

Savala leaned over, folding his long arms and propping his bony elbows on the table. He'd passed his mother in height a few months earlier, and he just kept growing. "I stepped in some mud on my way home," he began, "so I stopped at the well and took my boots off to rinse them. But then I stepped on a thorn."

Kari's face twisted. "One of the big ones?"

"Yes. But, Mother, there's more. I pulled it out, and it was bleeding, so I held it tight. Then my hands started to glow."

"Mmm hmm?" Kari was used to that; Savala's hands often glowed. And he wasn't the only one.

Sometimes, Kari's infant patients didn't breathe when they were born. Kari always shared her breath with those babies, just as she had with Savala. Ten years earlier, one such baby had been born facing up —again, just like Savala. After Kari had breathed in that baby's mouth, the newborn's chest had begun to glow with the same golden light that had filled Savala's chest at birth. This time, the light had moved into the child's eyes before fading away.

Since then, when a baby was born face-up, Kari asked the mother's permission to give that child a breath of air. Each time, the child glowed somewhere—ears, nose, eyes, mouth, hands, feet, or scalp. And all of those children, like Savala, continued to occasionally experience the same glow.

The golden light seemed pointless, but it gave Kari joy, reminding her of the magic she'd experienced during her months in the forest. Since Savala's birth, she hadn't heard one credible story of Sava sending his magic to help someone. Magic itself seemed to have died when Savala was born. At least the strange, golden glow reminded them that there was still something more than the ordinary world around them.

"Mother?"

Savala was waving his hand in front of Kari's face. She laughed. "I told you, I'm tired. I was daydreaming. Continue your story."

"As I said, my hand glowed, and then it felt warm—almost uncomfortable. When I pulled it away from my foot, well . . ." He pulled his foot up to his opposite knee and then lifted it to the table, showing it to his mother.

"Savala, get your foot off the table!"

He ignored her admonishment. "Look, Mother!"

She looked at the dirty sole of his foot. "Where was the thorn?"

He pointed, but the skin was unmarred. Kari looked up at him, knowing her question was written across her face. What was he saying?

"I think I healed my foot."

Kari's mouth hung open for a few silent seconds. She closed it, opened it again, and found she still had no words. So she stood and picked up a small paring knife off the countertop.

"Why do you have a knife?" Savala asked.

"Let's can you see if you can do it again."

He raised his eyebrows and nodded slowly.

Kari sat and pressed the knife against her forearm. She squeezed her eyes shut and drew in a sharp breath as she gave herself a tiny cut. Holding her hand in a tight fist, she reached her bleeding arm out to her son.

"What now?" Savala asked.

"Put your hand on my cut. Like you did with your foot."

Savala did, grimacing as his hand covered Kari's wound. A few seconds later, both his hands glowed, and the gentle, golden light illuminated his face, which was frozen in calm concentration.

Suddenly, Kari gasped and covered her mouth with her free hand. Her skin was moving under her son's touch, and the sharp pain from the cut was fading.

When Savala lifted his hand, Kari's arm was still bloody, but the cut was gone. They lifted wide eyes to meet each other.

"What is it?" Savala asked. "What's causing it?"

"It's a gift from Sava." For some reason, Kari was whispering. "Son, it's magic. It didn't leave the world after all. It's in you."

"Magic." That gentle smile overtook his face again.

A deep voice interrupted them. "What's this about magic?"

Kari looked up to find her husband walking through the doorway. He stopped next to them, leaning down and giving Kari a kiss on the cheek.

Kari reached out and took his hand and her son's, squeezing both. She found her husband's gaze and held it. "Oh, Dom," she said, "I think everything is about to change."

A NOTE FROM BETH

Thanks for reading *Birth of Magic*! Will you take a minute to write a short review at your online bookseller or on Goodreads? It's a great way to let me know if you'd like me to keep writing books like these— and to help others find this story.

Want more of this enchanting world? Check out The Sun-Blessed Trilogy, starting with *Facing the Sun*! You'll love the story of Tavi Malin, a girl with unstoppable magic.

Check out my second series, The Magic Eaters Trilogy. It's post-apocalyptic YA fantasy with some romance on the side—and I think you'll love it as much as I do. Download the first four chapters of *The Frost Eater*, Book 1, at bit.ly/FrostSneakPeek.

PREVIEW OF FACING THE SUN

SUN-BLESSED TRILOGY BOOK 1

Prologue

I remember that birth with more clarity than any other I attended. Even inconsequential details of that home, on that day, are written on my memory with indelible ink. Running, squealing children playing in front of the house as I arrived. The smell of freshly cut wood piled by the front door. Soot stains on the wall around the fireplace, the knot in the floorboard I felt through my shoe, the squeak of the front door as it was thrown open.

At first I didn't recognize the girl who answered my knock. We stared at one another for a long moment before I exclaimed, "Misty!"

She was twelve years old, and it seemed that overnight, she had become a young woman. But when she gave me that big smile of hers and said, "I think the baby is a girl," she again looked like the child I knew.

I returned Misty's smile then waved to her father, who had fetched me from the midwife house. Jevva took the gesture as permission to leave. He would go fishing during this birth as he did each time his wife was in labor. I think he could not bear to see her in pain. With her father gone, Misty brought me to the bedroom where her mother waited. She then returned to her siblings outside.

I entered Mey's room, and she opened her arms. Embracing her, I whispered, "Hello, strong mother." At that moment, a birth pain hit, and she held onto me, pressing her head into my chest and swaying. It was clear her labor was already advanced.

When the pain passed, Mey turned to me in tears. "I'm glad you're here," she told me. It is those four words that brought me into midwifery. I love babies, but I chose my profession because I love women. Mey's six older children had all been born into my hands, and she had long ago claimed a special spot in my heart.

Soon after I arrived, Mey began to talk through the pain, as she had done during every one of her labors. "Ohhh, my child, come," she said, her voice rhythmic, vowels extended. "You know what to do. You were made for this. Come, child, come." It makes me smile, even now—that sweet invitation, a cry of pain and love.

The morning passed in the timeless manner characteristic of labor. The pains continued to strengthen, and in between two of them, I asked Mey my favorite question for a laboring mother. "What is your hope for this child?"

She did not even have to think about the answer. "I hope my child is kind," she said, "and I hope my child is strong." She paused and added, "And I know I shouldn't hope for it, but I have always wanted one of my children to be born facing the sun."

I smiled. "Nearly every mother shares that desire," I said, palpating her abdomen to determine her child's position. "From what I can tell, this baby is facing your side. Likely it will turn to face the earth before emerging, and that is the easiest position—for you and for baby."

Mey glanced out the window toward her six other children, all of whom had been born without complication, face-down. I knew as soon as her child was born, Mey would be filled with such joy, she would forget she'd hoped for a sun-blessed babe.

The house became stuffier and warmer as the afternoon wore on, and at some point Mey began leaning out the window between her pains, her arms folded against the sill, the summer breeze cooling her skin. Even now I can picture her face, still so young, lit by a slight smile as the wind tangled her hair.

It was through this window that Mey heard two of her younger children bickering. She was breathing deeply through a difficult pain. As it diminished, she spoke in a voice so low, I had to get close to hear her. "Please tell them if they don't stop," she said, "they may not survive the afternoon." Suppressing a laugh, I repeated those exact words to them, and they ran off as quickly as their small legs could carry them.

Not long after that, Mey lifted her gown over her head, threw it on the bed, and continued to pace. Any modesty had faded away during hours of purposeful agony. And why should she be ashamed? Mey, pacing naked in her bedroom, was lovely. As every mother is.

I suspected Mey's sudden lack of reserve signaled a progression in her labor. Sure enough, when the next pain hit, the sounds coming from her mouth changed. Words had long ago become moans, and now moans became grunts, arising from deep within her. When the pain passed, I asked, "Time to push?"

"Yes," she said, her voice both determined and desperate.

"Good," I said. And when I smiled at her, her tired face found the strength to smile back.

On the next pain, Mey turned, putting both her hands on my shoulders, guiding me to my knees as she squatted in front of me. She held onto me as if I were the one tree still standing in a storm, and as she pushed, she roared.

But though Mey was ready, her child was not. It had been years since Mey had needed to push more than a few times to birth a child, but an hour passed, then another half hour, and still her baby did not emerge.

Mey's pushing continued with little progress. When I saw discouragement taking hold of her, I summoned my gift. Magic filled my hands, glowing with a golden light. I touched Mey's tense shoulders. In seconds, she was awash in peace, and she was ready for the next pain—or at least as ready as any expectant mother can be.

As I pulled my hands away and released my magic, there was a soft tap on the door. "Mama? Can I come in?"

Mey told me to open the door, and Misty entered. She did not talk to her mother. Instead, placing her hands on Mey's rounded abdomen, Misty spoke to the child inside. "I'm your sister. We're all so excited to meet you. I can't wait to hold you and teach you things. I'll always be there for you." And I believed her, believed she would do anything for the child that was coming.

Misty left, and I saw great peace on her mother's face. Yes, my magic had comforted Mey, but Misty's visit had helped her even more. Her oldest child had reminded Mey that her youngest child would be born into a family characterized by love.

Still the labor continued. I was as surprised as Mey when the gold and crimson light of sunset filled the sky. Her pains had begun before sunrise, and now I was lighting lanterns. Mey had by then been pushing for three hours.

She looked at the sky and said one word. "Beautiful." Then, as if the dying sun had renewed her strength, Mey pushed harder than she had in hours, and my hands at last guided the child's head out of its mother's body.

Mey's eyes, which had been glazed, burst to life again. Her teeth, which had ground together in effort, separated in a joyful smile.

But I could not speak. The head that had just emerged was still covered in its bag of waters. And Mey could not see that yet. Nor could she see the child's face, pressed against the sac that had been its home. Face-up. Facing the sun.

Mey examined my face, and her expression shifted from triumph to concern. "Is everything all right? Is the baby well?"

I gathered my wits and smiled. "Yes, all is well. On the next pain, you will hold your baby, and it will be born in its bag of waters."

With an expression of awe, Mey touched her child's head, covered in the smooth sac. I don't quite believe any of the old traditions about a baby born en caul. I didn't expect that Mey's child would be more fortunate than any other, or would be a strong swimmer. But such a birth seemed extra-miraculous, the infant reminding us of its mysterious first home, within a sac in its mother's womb.

When the next pain swelled, my hands guided the baby out of its mother, into the warm summer air. Mey watched in awe as I pulled the sac off the child's face and body. I then handed the slippery babe to its mother. Heedless of the dirty floor, of her nakedness, of the fluid puddling under her, of everything except the new creation she had just birthed, Mey brought her newest child to her chest. The room filled with the cries of mother and baby.

Mey exclaimed, "I have a daughter!" I laughed; I had not even thought to check, so focused had I been on removing the sac and on the child's position at birth.

I touched Mey's shoulder. "There is something else I want to tell you," I said. "Your daughter"—and my voice caught; this moment never got old—"your daughter was born facing the sun."

Mey froze for a moment. Then she was again crying, and she pulled me to her in an embrace, the baby, now quiet, between us. "She is sun-blessed?" Mey asked. "Truly?"

"En caul and sun-blessed. What a lovely birth. What a special child."

Mey was so focused on her new baby; she was barely aware of me as I cut the child's cord. Then I spoke. "You did your part beautifully today," I told her. "It's time for me to do mine."

She handed me her daughter and watched in wonder as I held the baby face-up on my forearm, head cradled in my hand. Light from a lantern fell on us, and the little one promptly squeezed her eyes shut. "Sun-blessed child," I said in a low voice, "in the name of Sava, who giveth the breath of life, I give thee the breath of blessing."

My mouth covered the infant's nose and mouth, and her tiny chest rose as my breath entered her lungs.

After she received her blessing breath, the baby's chest glowed with a strong, golden light that put the lantern to shame. The glow spread up her neck, up both cheeks, and then around her eyes, like a mask. "She is sight-blessed," I said, and Mey laughed with joy.

I opened my mouth to tell Mey what she might expect as her child grew, but the words stopped in my throat as I saw the glow on the baby's chest spreading again—this time down her legs and into her feet, all the way to the tips of her toes. "Stride-blessed as well," I said. Excitement filled the air between Mey and me. Twice-blessed!

And then I did not know where to look, because the golden light moved in all directions: down her arms, to her hands. Up the sides of her neck, to her ears. Up the front of her neck, then filling her lips, her nose. It was as if the glow were itself alive, breathing, spreading under the child's skin. As suddenly as it had started, the movement stopped, and I forgot to breathe as I lifted the babe, supporting her head, examining all sides of her. There was no part of her that was not glowing golden, from the bottoms of her feet to every strand of hair, which shone through its blackness.

My arms jolted when the newborn wailed again, and I handed her to her mother, who looked as if she didn't know whether to cry or sing or faint. Instinct took over, and Mey held the baby's mouth to her breast. The infant suckled greedily. As she ate, the glow faded, and she looked like any newborn eating her first meal.

Mey and I raised our heads to look in each other's eyes. She wet her lips with her tongue. "What . . . Why . . . ?" was all she could manage.

"I don't know," I said. "I don't know."

One question filled my mind: *Who is this child?*

-From *Midwife Memoirs* by Ellea Kariana

Want more? Get *Facing the Sun* on paperback, audiobook, or e-book now!

ABOUT THE AUTHOR

Carol Beth Anderson is a native of Arizona and now lives in Leander, TX, outside Austin. She has a husband, two kids, a miniature schnauzer, and more fish than anyone knows what to do with. Besides writing, she loves baking sourdough bread, knitting, and eating cookies and cream ice cream.

facebook.com/carolbethanderson

twitter.com/CBethAnderson

instagram.com/CBethAnderson

bookbub.com/profile/carol-beth-anderson

ACKNOWLEDGMENTS

As is the case with all books, creating *Birth of Magic* was a team effort!

I used Kickstarter to fund the paperback version of this book. My sincere thanks go to everyone who backed the project: Kendall Burn; Kim Clark, Tucson, AZ; Alain Davis; Kim Decker; Bert Edens; Erin; Jeff Gole, John Krugman (Hastcoat); Emerson Kasak; Sarah Lentz; Sheri Mayo; Tracy Mercer; Kris Newton; Becki Norris; Sean Norris Westmont; Renee Thompson; Toni Wall; and Garrett Wertz.

I have a small, trustworthy group of alpha readers. These brave souls read very early versions of the manuscript, full of grammatical errors and plot holes. Then they tell me (in marvelously helpful, gentle ways) how the book can be better. I can't thank them enough. Big, tight, digital hugs go to Ana Anderson, Eli Anderson, Becky Reed Brickman, Kim Decker, Melissa Lavaty, Stephanie Lynn, Becki Norris, Cathy Norris, Alex Pollnow, and DeDe Pollnow. (Special thanks to Becki, who suggested the scene with Dom visiting Kari in her room. It's one of my favorite parts of the book!)

After I've made big revisions, I send a manuscript to beta readers, who read a more-polished-yet-still-imperfect version. I got so much fantastic feedback, including massively helpful constructive criticism, from the *Birth of Magic* beta team! My heartfelt thanks go to every one of you: Danielle Ancona, Mackenzie Bitz, Becky Reed Brickman, Mary Cardwell, Alain Davis, Kim Decker, E, JoAnn Eaton, Brenda Elliott, Anastasia Forrest, Jennifer Fox, Lisa Henson, Cindy H., Brooke Hunger, Nathaniel Kaine, Tracy Magouirk, Kris Newton, Anne Perrault, Gilda Rodriguez, Indigo Smith, Renee Thompson, Nikki Tuggy, and Toni Wall.

I love using creative character names in fantasy novels, but sometimes I have a hard time thinking of all those names myself! I'm so grateful to those who suggested names of *Birth of Magic* characters: Monique Nadeau (Yolin), Jonah Kramer (Rusk), and my daughter Ana Anderson (Mara).

Thank you to Mariah Sinclair (mariahsinclair.com and thecovervault.com) for doing the gorgeous text on the cover and converting the e-book cover to a beautiful paperback version!

Thank you to Sonnet Fitzgerald (sonnetfitzgerald.com) for being such a thoughtful editor with an eye for detail and a heart of gold!

Thank you to God, who is the source of all the magical parts of my life—my family, my wonderful friendships, and my love of writing.

And readers, thank you for helping make my hours at the computer worth it!

-Carol Beth Anderson
Leander, Texas
2019